J. T. EDSON'S
FLOATING OUTFIT

The toughest bunch of Rebels that ever lost a war, they fought for the South, and then for Texas, as the legendary Floating Outfit of "Ole Devil" Hardin's O.D. Connected ranch.

MARK COUNTER was the best-dressed man in the West: always dressed fit-to-kill. **BELLE BOYD** was as deadly as she was beautiful, with a "Manhattan" model Colt tucked under her long skirts. **THE YSABEL KID** was Comanche fast and Texas tough. And the most famous of them all was **DUSTY FOG**, the ex-cavalryman known as the Rio Hondo Gun Wizard.

J. T. Edson has captured all the excitement and adventure of the raw frontier in this magnificent Western series. Turn the page for a complete list of Berkley Floating Outfit titles.

J. T. EDSON'S
FLOATING OUTFIT
WESTERN ADVENTURES
FROM BERKLEY

J.T. Edson

APACHE RAMPAGE

BERKLEY BOOKS, NEW YORK

Originally published in Great Britain by Brown Watson Ltd.

This Berkley book contains the complete
text of the original edition.
It has been completely reset in a typeface
designed for easy reading and was printed
from new film.

APACHE RAMPAGE

A Berkley Book / published by arrangement with
Transworld Publishers Ltd.

PRINTING HISTORY
Brown Watson edition published 1963
Corgi edition published 1969
Berkley edition / May 1984
Second printing / April 1987

ISBN: 0-425-09714-5

A BERKLEY BOOK ® TM 757,375
Berkley Books are published by The Berkley Publishing Group,
200 Madison Avenue, New York, New York 10016.
The name "BERKLEY" and the stylized "B" with design
are trademarks belonging to Berkley Publishing Corporation.

PRINTED IN THE UNITED STATES OF AMERICA

CONTENTS

CHAPTER ONE

Medicine Show

The wagon showed up like a black sheep on a snow-bank against the dull greys, browns and greens of the Dragoon Mountains. Originally it had been one of the big, four-horse, covered wagons which made the great cross-continental trails, taking travelers from the East to California. Instead of the canvas-covered top the sides were now made of wood, squarely built. The right side was made in two pieces, the outer of stout wood, serving as a stage, for this was a medicine show wagon. On the false side and the real sides, in glaring red, gold-edged letters, against the yellow of the wood, was emblazoned a message to the world.

"DOCTOR ERAZMUS K. THORNETT'S SUPERIOR
ELIXIR PRESENTS
MADAM FIONA .... World's Strongest Woman
THE MASKED MARKSWOMAN .... With Her Rifles
MAGDALENE AND SHARON .... Acrobats
Janice .... With Songs You Love To Hear
Rosemary .... Graceful, Artistic Dancing"

With its red-spoked wheels to augment the other

colors the wagon made quite a vivid splash in the foot-hills of the Dragoon Mountains. It was no more or less garish-looking than any other medicine show and offered a better selection of entertainment than most. The owner of the show, Doctor Erazmus K. Thornett presented an air of sober respectability to the wagon. It was an air which never really deserted him, not even while out on the trail, wearing an old, collarless shirt and trousers.

In town, dressed in his stylish, though just a little old-fashioned, black cutaway coat, fancy vest and elegant white trousers, he oozed respectability and confidence. His rather pompous, sun-reddened face and white hair helped his appearance. Even the fact that he always carried a Merwin and Hulbert army pocket revolver in a shoulder holster, did nothing to detract from his appearance. Rather it gave him an added touch of respectability and poise, a kind of dignity. It showed him as a gentleman who must be prepared to defend his life, property and honor in a hard land.

Taken all in all it would have come as a shock to many people that this elegant, learned-looking and educated-talking man was not a qualified doctor and never even attended any formal school of medicine. That did not make Doc Thornett a complete quack for he'd been thoroughly taught in the medicine show arts by a doctor who was struck from the rolls. Thornett could diagnose most ills which came his way and knew the best cures for all of them. He was an acknowledged expert of setting bones and removing bullets, two of the Western doctors' most common duties. He also pulled teeth with as little pain as possible, and there were several children who came into the world aided by his skilled attention.

So, even though his Superior Elixir was not the omnipotent cure-all he claimed it to be, he himself served a useful purpose. His medicine was harmless, did not taste bad, his show entertained and most folks thought they were getting their money's worth out of both. In the West there were few doctors, and at times Thornett served a very useful purpose, for he traveled to small villages where regular doctors but rarely came.

"We're headed for the wrong place this time, Doc," said the woman who sat by Thornett's side on the wagon box.

"And why, Phyllis me dove?"

Phyllis Lanley was anything but dove-like in appearance. She was a good-looking woman in her late thirties, middle-sized and stockily built. There was a tanned, healthy, happy air about her and her body, although plump looking, was hard and firm fleshed without any fat. Her red hair still was its own color and untouched by any aids against the greying of time, her skin was losing the youthful texture but not much. She wore an old shirtwaist which was strained by her swelling bust, her old jeans were tight at her hips, her arms and feet bare. The arms were strong looking, and hard muscles rolled under the skin, for she was Madam Fiona, the strong woman. Naturally strong, judicious fakery helped Phyllis to appear even stronger when she did her act. Her four daughters were the rest of the cast. They were in the back of the wagon and dressed in the same way as their mother.

Three of the girls leaned on the back of the wagon box, looking over Phyllis and Thornett's shoulders. Molly, the oldest girl was at the right. She was a plump red-haired girl, pretty and talented. She was the Masked Markswoman and Magdalene of the acrobatic act, good at both and a possible successor to her mother's crowd-drawing act. In the center was Patty, red-haired, pretty, hot-tempered and slim; she appeared as Sharon and was a skilled contortionist. Rosemary, or Rosie as she was always called by the others, stood at the left. She was a slim, good-looking blonde, pleasant, a good dancer, but by far the most naive of the girls.

The last of the girls, Rosie's twin sister, Janice, was inside the wagon. She sat on the lid of a box which contained the troupe's costumes, reading the words of a new song. Janice was blonde, plump and the best-looking of the girls. She was also the most house-proud. It was Janice who, besides her singing, took care of the affairs of the troupe. The others helped with the chores but Janice was the only one who gave any thought to the state of the food supply, or the purchasing and repair of clothing. Her voice was very good, and Thornett hoped one day to get her on the legitimate stage.

The towns the show played were rough, raw, rugged and proud of the boast that they'd never been curried below the knees. The men were fighters, the saloon girls and poorer townswomen, proud of their ability in a hair-yanking battle. So Phyllis became a bare-knuckle boxer and later added the claim that she was Champion of the World. A strong woman's act was an open challenge to the rough girls of the towns, and Phyllis learned to look after herself.

Even though he would rather not have been going for the fight, Thornett was not sorry to leave Tucson behind. The town was too big and civilized these days. A town with two resident doctors and a dentist was of no use to Thornett, for people tended to go to them rather than to him. Out at Fort Owen it would be different; the soldiers were cut off from civilization and would welcome a visit from the show. It was more than likely they would want to bet on their challenger, so Thornett was planning to make a stop at Baptist's Hollow and raise some extra cash.

The wagon, pulled by the four big, matched black horses, was following the main stage-coach route. Route was a grandiloquent name for the scar left by the wheels of many vehicles. It followed the smoothest, easiest route, one once used by Apache war parties and there were few better natural surveyors of land than the Apache. On either side rolled off barren land, marred by stinkwood, cholla, cactus and prickly pear. Even the sparse grass looked yellowish and unpalatable to animals. All in all the landscape looked what it was, a hard, harsh, raw land. Until only a couple or so years ago it was the roaming land of the Apache nation.

Looking around her Phyllis felt a dislike for the land. There was none of the rich, lush green of the Texas cattle country or the orderly neatness of the farm lands of the Mississippi. This country was harsh and unpleasant compared with either of them. For all that Phyllis would rather be out here than in the town of Baptist's Hollow.

"Let just collect supplies, Doc," she suggested. "We needn't take the wagon in. Janice and I can walk in and bring out all we'll need to get us to Fort Owen without taking the wagon."

"Most certainly not, me dear. Our good friends, Sergeants Magoon and Tolitski, will have money to wager on your fistic encounter and we can always use money. Can we not?" Thornett said pompously, beaming at Phyllis. "The more we wager the more we will win, without the risk of coming too close to the proverbial blanket in the inconceivable event of your losing the pending bout of fisticuffs. True, money does little or nothing to purchase happiness, yet it goes far to allowing one to be miserable in comfort.''

Phyllis laughed as she heard Thornett once more expressing his views on the subject of money. She knew it was no use trying to dissuade him once his mind was made up. Yet Phyllis did not relish the idea of going into the hostile town, for hostile she knew it would be. There'd been other hostile towns in their travels, they'd been won over by Thornett's eloquence or the show. This town was different, it wanted no part of them and would treat them as undesirable aliens.

CHAPTER TWO

Baptist's Hollow

The town lay in the steep sided protection of a U-shaped draw, back from the main stage trail. Access to the town by wagon or stage-coach was only possible through the open end of the U, the sides being too steep-sloped even for a man to ride a horse down. From the main stage route the trail branched down and at the city limits became Church Street, main and only thoroughfare of the town. Along Church Street has most of the town's business section; stores, the one saloon, the town court offices which also housed the Marshal's office and jail, the Wells Fargo depot and the telegraph office. The Wells Fargo office was the sole reason for the town being here at all. It served as the main relay point for the stage-coaches.

There were few people on the street as the garish-looking medicine show wagon entered the town. Phyllis watched the few who were on the street, noting the disapproval on their faces. The men all seemed to be wearing sober black suits and low crowned black hats. The women were dressed in black frocks which hid any sign of womanhood. On every face was a look of miserable

7

piety which would have warned off a more sensitive man than Thornett.

Looking around him, Thornett was supremely confident that the people would thaw out when they saw the show. It was all good, clean fun, but for all that he was pleased he'd remembered to warn Rosie to cut out her rather risque can-can for this one show. He knew his persuasive tongue well and was sure he could soothe the most disapproving crowd. For all that he was startled by the scowls which greeted his warm and friendly hat-raising.

"Doc! Hey, Doc Thornett!"

The voice brought them to a halt outside the town courthouse. At a barred window of the jail Thornett saw two familiar faces. One was a cheery, sun—or whisky—reddened face with twinkling brown eyes. The other was a thinner set of features, rather vacant and dreamy-looking. He recognized them both, and although it did not surprise him to see them framed by a set of bars, he was surprised to find them jailed in so small a town.

Always polite, Thornett raised his hat in a friendly greeting. "Good morning to you, Scully old friend. How are you today, and you, Willy?"

"Howdy, Doc, Miz Phyllis," replied the simple-looking, tow-headed, younger face, beaming delightedly. "Ain't seed you all in a coon's age."

Thornett was curious, though not unduly worried at seeing Scully and Willy in jail. They were a pair of confidence tricksters who made their living selling gold bricks, fortune telling and otherwise extracting money from the gullible. Scully was a brash, jovial, fast-talking man who always dressed well, and ran the team. Willy was a gangling, raw-boned young man who looked like a half-wit and talked with a slow southern drawl. His talk and appearance acted as a blind, for Willy was far from being the fool he looked. When needed he was far from slow, could swing a punch like a Missouri mule's kick and fight like a tiger. His big, awkward-looking hands were capable of delicate manipulations with a deck of cards. Not only could he deal the second or bottom card with ease, but he was a master of the most difficult move in the cheater's repertoire. He could remove a desired card from the center of the deck without being detected. It was his general slow appearance which acted as a cover when his talents were being put to use.

"How do you come to be incarcerated in this small and undeveloped town?" Thornett asked, although he could guess.

Scully sounded more indignant than distressed at his plight. "Like this, Doc. I thought the rubes here would go for the Old John Conquer Root and was just starting to tell them how it cures all ills, makes child birth easy and restored vitality to men, when the great seizer arrived. You know I abhor violence, especially when there's a ten-gauge lined on me. So we came along quietly. We're in jail for offending public morals and for vagrancy. What's more, that sick marshal won't take a bribe." From Scully's tone this was the supreme indignity of all. "Imagine that, a hick town marshal who can't be making more than thirty dollars a month clear, tossing me in the hoosegow *and* refusing to accept a bribe. Why, I've bribed such exponents of the badge as Wyatt Earp, Wild William Hickok and Jim Court-right in my time, always doing it in such a way as to give no offense. And this hick refuses to accept one. More, he says he'll hold me for attempting to bribe an official if I try it again."

"Hard luck, Scully," said Phyllis, smiling now she knew the jailing was not on a serious charge.

Scully nodded his thanks to Phyllis. He'd known Thornett's show for several years and early on made an attempt on Phyllis's virtue. Her refusal and his failure made him respect her all the more. He gave a warning to his friends:

"I wouldn't show here, was I you, Doc. Not unless you and the girls want to join me here. And I warn you the food's terrible. This town's no good."

"Thanks for the warning, old friend," replied Thornett. "Do you have sufficiency of the wherewithal to purchase your release, to whit, by payment of your fine?"

"Sure, we'll get by, thanks," answered Scully. He knew Thornett would make the offer and was grateful, but he would never take money from a good friend when he did not need it. "You get out of here while you can."

Thornett started the wagon forward again, seeing the "I told you so" look on Phyllis's face. He was not unduly worried by Scully's warning, even though the conversation did not go unnoticed by the watching people. Scully was a confidence trickster. His entire way of business was different from Thornett's. The medicine show gave folks a good entertainment for their money and made no attempt to cheat them.

There was no way the wagon could turn in the street. Even the stage-coaches were compelled to enter the plaza to make a turn. So Thornett drove on, sublimely unconscious of the angry looks and morose mutterings of the gathering people. He knew they were following the wagon and thought they were coming to see his show. Phyllis and the girls saw the crowd following and did not feel so happy about it. The girls stood at the rear of the wagon, looking through the window in the door. Molly turned and loaded both her rifles. She'd seen too many hostile crowds not to see the signs. There was no enthusiasm or interest in those miserable-looking faces, only cold dislike and disapproval.

Bringing his wagon into the plaza, Thornett beamed in delight. The place was almost made for his show. He brought the team around and halted them on the far side in front of the church. Jumping down, he expected the girls to come and help him get ready. Usually Phyllis and Molly lowered the stage while Patty fixed on the supports for it and the younger girls started to ready the equipment for the show. Not one of the women moved. Phyllis sat on the wagon box and watched the people who were now crossing the plaza, standing well clear of the wagon, to watch every move the show people made.

"Janice, me dear," said Thornett, looking in some surprise at Phyllis and the girls. This was a team job, and they did not hang back from it at other times. "Get your guitar and entertain the good people whilst the rest of us make ready. We've an audience and nothing to show them."

"That's no audience, Doc," warned Phyllis. "It looks more like a lynch mob to me. Let's forget it and move on."

"Nonsense, me dove. True, they appear a touch soggy and dull, but I'll toss 'em a few nifties which will tickle their sense of humor better than a goose-feather. They'll probably turn into quite a warm and appreciative audience before we get through with them."

Phyllis doubted that. From the looks of the crowd, it would only be responsive when the marshal either took the show to jail or chased it out of town. She saw the faces of two women in particular among the others. One was thin, narrow and sharp, a mean face. The other was far, bloatedly fat, yet it was not a happy-fat face. These two seemed even more vicious and hating than the others.

"Look there, Mrs. Haslett," the fat woman said in a loud voice which carried to Phyllis. "That man's got four women with him."

"Just goes to show what sort of folks they are, don't it, Mrs. Millet," replied the thin one maliciously.

Phyllis's face flushed red at the words. The insult did not annoy her for her own sake, but for the implied slur on the innocent Doc and her daughters. It was at that moment Phyllis decided the time had come when she must take the initiative and persuade Doc to marry her. That would put things on a basis where such remarks could not be made. Right now it was more important that they got out of town, and she opened her mouth to say so.

A man was coming along Church Street, stepping through the crowd on the plaza. The people made way for this man, allowed him through, then moved up behind him.

He was a big man, tall, wide-shouldered and hard-looking. His face showed some strength, it was a hard face and one without the saving grace of humor about it. On his head was a Union Army officer's campaign hat. His clothes were of the same sober black. Unlike the majority of the men in the crowd, he wore a gunbelt. A fast man's rig from the look of it. The holster was low-hanging, tied to his leg, the side cut away to allow the trigger-finger to find the guard of the revolver. It was the rig a good man with a gun would wear. The old range saying went, "A man who ties down his holster doesn't talk much—not with his mouth."

Phyllis watched the man. She did not need to see the marshal's badge to know who he was. This was the great seizer, the man who shipped a dance-hall girl back to Tucson without letting her walk on the streets of the town. This was the man who threw Scully and Willy into jail on a charge of offending public morality. She knew who he reminded her of and did not like the comparison. There was a look about him which reminded her of Wyatt Earp. Yet this man was different from Earp in one respect. He would not take a bribe, whereas the rumor was strong that Earp not only would, but often did.

Thornett studied the crowd as they moved forward. They were far less enthusiastic than he'd expected, but he was prepared to win them over as he'd won over many another town from here to California and back the long way.

"Greetings, good citizens of the fair town of Baptist's Hollows," he began. "I am here today with a rare and exciting offer which may never come your way——"

"You've got just fifteen minutes to get out of town."

Thornett halted his speech as the words came from the town marshal. He frowned and threw the man a look which had quelled many a frontier bully. There was no apparent effect this time.

"I beg your pardon, my good man. May I ask you to repeat that most extraordinary remark."

"I said you'd got fifteen minutes to get out of town. See you're gone."

"Now see here, my man," boomed Doc, eyebrows fluffing angrily and face reddening in indignation. "I have come out of my way, at considerable expense, I would add, to include this town on my itinerary. I would be obliged if you——"

"You heard what I said," snapped the marshal, stopping Thornett's tirade. "We don't want your kind in this town."

"Kind sir, *kind*!" Thornett replied, ignoring the muttered agreement with the marshal's words. He could also see that Phyllis had been right all along but did not mean to give up without a fight. "You make it appear the West is full of purveyors of my Superior Elixir. I assure you that this is far from being so."

"Cut it out," the marshal's voice dropped to an angry growl. "I've told you how long you've got here and ——"

Doc knew his sole remaining hope was to talk the other man down and do it fast. "Do you suffer from aches and pains, my good public servant? Or are you a martyr to indigestion? If so, allow me to present to you, free, gratis and without any cost at all, one of my Superior Elixirs. This potion of mine, handed down from an Indian medicine man——"

"Listen you," growled the marshal, in a tone which warned Thornett off. "One more word like that and I'll jail you for attempting to bribe a peace officer."

"Run them right out of town, Major Ellwood," screeched the thin woman. "We don't want that sort of rabble in our town."

The marshal turned and shook his head. "I gave them fifteen minutes and they've got a little less than that now. They aren't going to give their indecent show, but they might want to buy some supplies or something."

The thin woman looked as if she were torn between two conflicting emotions. Her husband owned the local store, and it would most likely be he who profited from any trade the medicine show brought. She also wanted to see the show chased out of town. Putting on a simpering smile that was reserved for important people like the marshal and the minister, she said:

"Well, I suppose we must show some charity. I just did not wish our young people to be corrupted by their kind."

That was the sort of thing Phyllis expected from people like these. They would not allow the show to perform but were willing to take its money. Apparently, taking Thornett's money would not endanger or corrupt anyone. She looked at Doctor Thornett who was now facing Ellwood, all puffed up like a bantycock.

"Come on, Doc," she said. "Let's get out of here."

"Major Ellwood'll see you do," jeered the fat woman. Her eyes showed her hatred and envy at any other woman who was better favored than herself. She hated Phyllis for looking younger, healthier and happier than herself.

"Now wait a minute, Mrs. Millet," a thin, mournful-looking man put in. "Like the major says, they might want to buy supplies."

Thornett ignored this. He fastened the knot he'd loosened ready to lower the stage. Then, with quiet dignity in every line of his frame, turned to run a final bluff on the marshal.

"I suppose you are aware that the mayor of the town is a personal friend of mine, my good man?" he asked. "And that he——"

For a bluff it missed by a good country mile. "I'm the mayor, and the town marshal," Ellwood answered. "You'd best get to moving, time's running out on you."

"Don't worry," snapped Phyllis, watching various

people consulting their watches. "We're going as soon as we turn the wagon."

"We need supplies, maw," Janice put in, coming forward.

"Don't we have enough to make Fort Owen?" Phyllis asked, not wishing to allow the people of Baptist's Hollow any profit from their show.

"Not unless you want to eat grass all the way."

"A most unpalatable source of nutriment, me dove," said Doc, climbing back on to the wagon. "Far less so than more normal human food." Taking out a notecase which drew avaricious eyes to it, Thornett extracted several bills and gave them to Janice. "Purchase a sufficiency to enable us to reach Fort Owen, my dear."

Taking the money Janice went through the wagon, opened the door and climbed down. In other towns there would have been plenty of young men willing to help her down. Here there was no such move. The young men in the crowd studiously avoided looking at the girl. The crowd parted to allow her through. Thornett started his horses moving, and drove slowly to give the girl time to make her purchases. At the water-trough on the side of the plaza, he halted the team and told the girls to water the horses. The crowd made no attempt now to either help or hinder. They just stood watching, blank unfriendly faces staring at everything the medicine show people did.

Janice walked through the crowd and along to Haslett's General Store. She pushed open the door and entered. The store might have called itself general, but it did not stock the wide range of other such places she'd seen. There was food for sale and a few cooking utensils, but none of the other wide range most general stores sold. The store was empty, except for a young man who was sweeping the floor. He put down the brush and came towards the girl. He was a tall, slim, good-looking man of perhaps twenty years. There was something about him, some look, which did not appear to belong to this town.

"Serve you, miss?" he asked.

"Sure," Janice replied, looking at the well-stocked shelves of canned goods. Quickly she gave him a list of what she wanted, and he went about filling the order with deft hands. All went well until she said, "I'd like four cans of peaches."

The peaches were right on the top shelf, and a ladder stood by for the purpose of bringing them down. The young man looked around him cautiously. Then, ignoring the ladder, he picked up his broom and knocked four cans off the shelf. They fell one after the other and he caught them as they dropped, each landing on the one preceding until he held all four on the palm of his right hand.

"Say, that was good," remarked Janice, for the move was slick, smooth and showed practice. "I'd like a couple of cans of tomatoes as well."

To her surprise the young man casually knocked down the required cans, catching them on top of the peaches. "Shucks, that wasn't nothing much at all," he said. Looking cautiously around once more, he dropped his voice. "You're with the traveling show, aren't you?"

"Sure," agreed Janice, waiting for either a sneer or an obscene suggestion.

Neither came. The young man looked friendly and delighted at meeting a member of a traveling show. He shot a scared glance at the door as if not wishing to be overheard in what he was going to say.

"I saw me a traveling show one time when I was in Tucson. Mr. Haslett took me in to do the heavy lifting. Left me while he went to the meeting house. So I slipped away and saw the show. Was a juggler in it and he was good. I come back home and tried to learn his tricks. I never let on to Mr. Haslett about it. He reckons all you show folks are sinners."

"He could be right," answered Janice.

"Shucks, I know what he is. That meeting house he went to—it had a red lamp hanging outside. Say, how'd you like me to show you a trick or two? They won't be back while there's a chance of seeing something."

"Sure, go ahead," Janice agreed tolerantly. She could see the young man was not happy living in Baptist's Hollow. No young man would be. He was going to need to leave soon, or wind up like the older men here. The sort of man who would sneak off to a joy house when well away from his home, but would demand that no such establishment be allowed in his home town. She did not wish to hurt the young man's feelings by refusing and so stood watching.

The young man placed her order in a sack, then took up six tomato cans. "My name's Elwin," he said as he began to throw the cans into the air and catch them as they fell. "The Hasletts took me in after the Apaches got my folks."

Took in would be the right word, Janice thought. The Hasletts did not appear to be the sort of folks who would perform any charitable action unless they saw a good return for the deed. Her attention went to the large, awkward cans as they flew through the air. Janice bit down an exclamation of surprise. She'd expected to see a simple trick. This was not simple. It was as good as any she'd ever seen on a stage. He ended the trick by catching them all one on top of the other.

"That was really good," said Janice.

Laying the cans back where they came from, Elwin picked six eggs from a basket and began juggling with them. Janice held her startled words down. Eggs were far from being conventional material for a juggler. She could see why he used such unusual props; they were all that came to his hands. Janice gasped as one of the eggs flew off at a tangent and, by an apparent accident, was caught again. All the time Elwin did his act he held his face in an expression of worried concern which amused the girl. He was a natural, talented and skilled. Given the right sort of coaching Elwin could go far as a juggler. Janice found herself wishing Thornett could see the act and give his opinion of it.

So absorbed were they that neither Janice nor Elwin saw the two faces which peered in the window. They did not see the medicine show wagon come to a halt outside the store either. Elwin juggled and Janice watched until the door was thrown open and an enraged feminine voice shrieked:

"Elwin!"

The six eggs went crashing to the floor, breaking and making a mess. Elwin's mouth dropped open. There was a guilty, furtive expression on his face as he turned to face the two women who entered the store.

"Yes, Mrs. Haslett?"

The thin woman, followed by the fat one, came in, slamming the door behind them. They both crossed the room to face Elwin and Mrs. Haslett hissed, "I've warned you before about wasting your time like that. Now I find you fooling about with this hussy and breaking my eggs."

"I'd throw that trollop out into the gutter where she

belongs, Mrs. Haslett,'' put in Mrs. Millet, secure in her extra size and weight. "The dirty little slut."

Janice was the most even-tempered of Phyllis's daughters. If Mrs. Millet had said such a thing about any of the others, particularly Patty, she'd have soon wished she kept her mouth tight shut. However, Janice held her temper for she knew anything she said would merely make it worse for Elwin. Taking out the money Thornett gave her, Janice put the price of the supplies on the counter and reached for the sack. She wanted to get out of the store before there was any trouble.

"Just a minute, you," snapped Mrs. Haslett, moving nearer. "You pay for the eggs Elwin bust."

For the first time in his life Elwin came out in open rebellion against the vinegar-tongued woman. "That's not right, Mrs. Haslett. It was me, not the young lady who broke the eggs."

"Young lady, is it?" Mrs. Haslett yelled. Backed by the hefty Mrs. Millet she was sure the girl would not dare object. "You keep your mouth shut."

"If anybody pays for the eggs it should be me," insisted Elwin.

"Why you ungrateful young wretch," Mrs. Haslett squealed. Words seemed to fail her at that moment, and she swung the flat of her hand hard against Elwin's face. The bony fingers left a red mark on his cheek.

Elwin took a step back, his face reddening with embarrassment at being struck in front of a stranger. Particularly in front of this pretty, friendly girl. Then he saw Janice lunge forward, going in front of him. There was an angry look on her face, the look of a female bobcat defending its young. Her voice was a low hiss, throbbing with fury.

"Don't lay a hand on him again."

Mrs. Haslett stepped back before the fury of the small girl. Mrs. Millet, feeling secure in her extra size and weight, swung her hand hard. Janice's head rocked to the slap, and she crashed into the bar by Elwin's side. Never in all his life had Elwin seen such a look as came into the girl's eyes. Janice appeared to be transformed into a savage, spitting hellcat, even as the big woman stepped forward to slap again. Without a sound Janice hurled herself at the big, fat woman.

For all her even temper Janice knew well enough how to take care of herself. She and the other girls sometimes found themselves involved in hair-tearing battles with jealous females of the towns they visited. Mostly Janice only joined in out of family feeling, but once in not even Patty could come to her for sheer fighting fury. Lowering her head, Janice ducked under Mrs. Millet's reaching hands to butt into the fat stomach. The fat woman gave a startled, pain-filled gasp and doubled over with hands clawing wildly at Janice's firm muscled body, but the girl was too fast for her. Swarming over Mrs. Millet and bringing the big woman crashing on to her back, Janice let loose the full flood of her temper, using feet, knees, fists, elbows and teeth to hurt the big woman. Mrs. Millet screamed and flailed her arms wildly, kicking her fat legs in a desperate effort to throw Janice from her. Without a sound Janice took a double handful of the woman's hair and began to smash her head against the hard boards of the floor.

Screaming in terror and rage, Mrs. Haslett moved forward, caught Janice by the hair from behind and pulled her from Mrs. Millet. Janice let out a howl of pain, the first time she'd made a sound. Her foot lashed back and caught the woman on the shin. Mrs. Haslett let Janice's hair free and howled, hopping on one leg.

Janice came round and hurled at the other woman, driving her back into the counter by the fury of her attack. Mrs. Millet got to her feet and lunged after the fighting pair. Her right hand caught Janice's frock and tore it, then they all tangled in a wild fighting mêleé.

Elwin stood pressed back against the bar, unable to do a thing. The fury of the fight scared him. He'd never seen women fight before, and the fury was far worse than anything he could imagine. The pretty, friendly little girl was now transformed into a wild-eyed, savage wildcat, for like most even people Janice was far worse than any bully when roused.

The three women staggered wildly across the floor and in a tangled mass hit the door, bursting it open and reeling out on to the sidewalk. Mrs. Haslett gripped Janice from behind, holding her while Mrs. Millet rained slaps at her face and head.

Phyllis came to her feet. She'd heard the noise in the store and was on the point of investigating when the three came into view. Even before Phyllis could make a move to go help her daughter it was too late. She felt a violent push, and saw a red-haired shape hurling over the wagon box. It was Patty. She'd seen her little sister in trouble and needing help. Patty was just the girl to hand out that same help.

Hurling over the wagon box Patty landed full on Mrs. Millet's back and the fat woman thought she'd been jumped by a pile of wildcats. Patty was bigger, stronger and even more skilled than her sister, for she was ready to fight at the drop of a hat. The big woman lit down on the sidewalk, managed to roll over and wished she had not, for Patty started to bounce her already sore and aching head on the sidewalk.

Mrs. Haslett saw what was happening to her friend

and showed true loyalty. She could barely hold the wildly struggling Janice, so let loose, pushed the girl away and turned to dash back into the store, slamming the door. Janice swung around and gave an angry yell, then started to lunge forward. Phyllis caught Janice by the arm and thrust her backwards. She saw the crowd running towards the scene and knew she must act fast to save her daughters from serious trouble. She'd followed Patty out of the wagon and darted by Janice to where Patty knelt astride the now still Mrs. Millet, slamming her head on the sidewalk. There was no time to speak, nor would it be any use when Patty's temper was up. Phyllis knotted her hand in her daughter's hair and heaved. Patty gave an angry yell as she hit the hitching rail by Janice. For a moment the red-head tensed to throw herself at her new attacker. Then she recognized her mother and relaxed. Turning to Janice she looked at the torn frock and the blood running from her sister's lip.

"You all right, Jan?"

Janice was breathing hard, she rubbed the blood, then nodded. "I'm all right now, Patty. Thanks."

"I'd do it any time," answered Patty.

Phyllis did not look at the still form on the sidewalk. She saw the crowd running forward and snapped an order for her girls to get into the wagon. There was not time. The crowd surrounded them in an ugly, angry mass.

CHAPTER THREE

Dead as a Six Day Stunk-Up Skunk

Ellwood burst through the menacing and advancing crowd. "Back off, all of you. Back off there!"

Mrs. Haslett opened the door about half an inch to peep out and make sure Janice was not waiting to grab her. Seeing the marshal and her friends gathered she came out, sniffing and dabbing the blood from her face. Stepping by the still form of Mrs. Millet, she advanced to the edge of the sidewalk.

"Those two sluts attacked poor Mrs. Millet and me," she sniffed.

Patty gave an angry hiss and turned from climbing into the wagon, but her mother caught and held her. With an angry growl Ellwood swung back his hand as if to hit the girl.

"Don't do that," snapped Thornett.

Turning, Ellwood opened his mouth to say something. His hand dropped towards his side then froze. Thornett's right hand went under his coat and came out holding the short-barreled Merwin and Hulbert gun. One of the crowd, one of the few who were armed, made a grab for his weapon with no greater success than

Ellwood. Molly saw the move and kicked open the rear
door of the wagon, her rifle slanting down at him and
ending the move undone.

"Put that gun away," Ellwood ordered. "I'm taking
you to jail."

Thornett shook his head gently and made no attempt
to holster the revolver. He could see the dull, ugly mood
of the crowd and knew things might go badly for the
girls if he allowed them to be taken. One thing he was
sure of now, Ellwood was not a good man with a gun.
The fighting man's gunbelt was nothing but a bluff.

"I'm afraid I must decline, my good public servant,"
Thornett answered. Even at such a time he still retained
his pompous way of talking. "Get into the wagon,
Phyllis, me dove. And you, girls."

"Stop them, Major," screamed Mrs. Haslett. "I
want them girls arrested for attacking me and poor Mrs.
Millet."

Ellwood frowned. He was being given a formal complaint and should act on it. There was only one thing
wrong. That gun was still lined on him, and there was a
look of determination on the medicine man's face. "Put
down that gun," he said.

"I'm afraid not. We're leaving right now."

"You're resisting arrest," warned Ellwood. "You
leave this town and I'll have you posted as a wanted
man."

Thornett neither lowered his gun, nor relaxed. He
doubted if Ellwood could post him as wanted or would
be willing to risk it. Not when a good lawyer could clear
Thornett on any of the charges without pausing to take
breath. However, it might prove inconvenient for him
and the show to have such a thing hanging over them. It

might be as well to straighten things out before he left.

"We'd like to know what did happen in the store," Thornett said, backing the suggestion with his lined gun. "I would suggest you find out before making threats of arrest, Marshal. There is such a thing as being sued for false arrest."

Ellwood knew this and growled out, "All right. What did happen in there, Mrs. Haslett?"

The woman opened her mouth, then closed it again. It was not easy to bring out the words in a manner which would be creditable to herself and Mrs. Millet. "They attacked poor Mrs. Millet and myself in there," she lied. "Both of them. When we caught them making up to Elwin."

"I wish to point out," Thornett put in, "that only Janice went inside. Patty remained in full view of all of you."

Mrs. Haslett gulped. She'd made a slip and could see Ellwood was not missing it. The town marshal frowned, knowing what was happening. Only one girl did go into the store, the other having been in sight of the wagon most of the time. He also knew the small girl would not willingly start trouble with two women, one almost twice as large as she was. He knew that, truth or lies from Mrs. Haslett, the crowd did not aim to see these people leave town.

Looking at Janice, who stood by her mother waiting for Patty to climb into the wagon, Ellwood said, "All right, tell me what happened."

"The big woman hit me after I stopped the other one hitting the boy who works inside. I hit her back and they both started on me."

"Liar!" shrieked Mrs. Haslett, then gave a scared

yelp as Janice lunged forward at her.

Catching her daughter's arm and shoving her against the wagon, Phyllis asked, "Why not get the young feller out here and ask him?"

"Elwin," called Ellwood. "Come on out here."

Elwin came from the store carrying Janice's sack of supplies. He put the sack on the edge of the sidewalk and turned to the marshal. "Yes, sir?"

"Tell us what happened in the store."

"This young lady come in to buy supplies, and I started to show her a couple of juggling tricks. Then Mrs. Haslett and Mrs. Millet came in. Mrs. Haslett started to abuse me and her. Then Mrs. Millet slapped her face and they both started on her."

"Why, of all the lying, ungrateful wretches——!" gasped Mrs. Haslett. She looked at the thin, miserable-looking man who was her husband. "Dudley, did you hear what he just said?"

Haslett gave a guilty start, for he was looking at Janice's half bared bust which showed from the torn frock. He turned his annoyance at the interruption on the young man. "Is that the sort of gratitude we get after taking you in and caring for you all these years?"

Elwin was on the rebellious trail and did not mean to be put on any more. He gave an angry cough of laughter. "Took me in and cared for me? That's a big joke. I worked twice as hard and four times as cheap as any hired man you could have got. The young lady wasn't doing a thing until those two started to abuse her."

"You make him shut his mouth, Major!" Mrs. Haslett screamed.

"That's fairness for you." Phyllis spat the words out. "If the young man'd said Janice was at fault he could have talked as much as he wanted."

"Shut your mouth unless I speak to you," Ellwood barked, "or I'll shut it for you."

For once the bombast left Thornett's voice. "Mister! You lay one hand on any of my young ladies and I'll kill you."

Once more Ellwood looked death in the face, for the plump, mild-looking man was in deadly earnest. The big marshal looked into his own motives, not liking what he saw. He did not have the cold-blooded courage necessary to go against a man holding a drawn, lined gun. More so when the man holding it was in the right.

The crowd was rumbling angrily although they also lacked the courage to go up against any armed person. They were willing to shove their marshal against those guns, even if they would not go up against the same guns. Ellwood listened to the rumble of the crowd and did not like what he heard. That was not the protest of a righteously outraged crowd; it was the snarl of a lynch mob. He knew that if he was able to arrest the show people, his trouble would not be over.

So interested in what was happening were the participants of the scene that none of them saw the four newcomers to the town. Four men had just come down from the stage trail and were now sitting their horses and watching everything.

They were young Texas cowhands, sat afork magnificent horses, one of them leading a pack-pony. Four Texas cowhands, three of them belting on a matched brace of Colt revolvers.

One of this quartet would have caught the eye in any crowd. He was a handsome blond giant, a rangeland dandy, yet a working cowhand or his expensive, made-to-measure clothes lied. Around his waist was a brown

leather, hand-tooled buscadero gunbelt supporting a
finely made brace of Colt Cavalry Peacemakers in the
holsters. He lounged easily in the saddle of his huge
bloodbay stallion, a light rider despite his great size.

The two men who flanked the handsome dandy
would also catch the eye. One of them sat a seventeen-
hand white stallion. He was tall, slim, lithe and dark
looking. His face looked young, almost babyishly
young and innocent, but those red-hazel eyes were
neither young nor innocent. His clothing was all black,
from hat to boots. Even the gunbelt was black leather.
Only the butt forward, walnut grips of the old Colt
Dragoon revolver at his right and the ivory hilt of the
bowie knife at his left relieved the blackness.

The other eye-catching man was younger, not out of
his teens. He sat astride a seventeen-hand paint stallion,
a fine-looking horse, and led the pack-pony. His clothing was expensive yet practical, like the dress of the
handsome giant. He was a blood youngster, handsome,
blue-eyed and friendly, and his face was strong, without
any trace of dissipation. Around his slender waist was a
new-looking gunbelt which carried the staghorn butted
Colt Artillery Peacemakers in the low-hanging holsters.

The fourth man sat slightly ahead of the others. He
lounged in the Texas kak saddle with the easy grace of a
cowhand. He was a small, insignificant man, the sort
who would go unnoticed in any crowd. Even the butt
forward, bone-handled Colt Civilian Peacemakers in
the holsters of his gunbelt did nothing to make him look
more noticeable. His clothes looked plain, but they were
costly, his black J. B. Stetson expensive as were his
high-heeled boots. He was a handsome enough young
man, but not in the eye-catching, attention-drawing way
of the golden-blond giant. Not in the lean, latently

savage, somehow Indian way of the dark-faced rider of the big white. Not in the friendly, clean and open way of the youngster. His face was handsome. It was also, if one took time out to look, a strong, commanding face. Sitting his huge paint stallion the small man thrust back his hat, showing his dusty blond hair as he looked at the wagon. His face flickered in a half smile as if he thought he knew the people in the medicine show.

"Let's get moving, Doc," said Phyllis, not seeing the riders, her full attention on the crowd.

Elwin stood on the sidewalk, watching. This was the supreme moment of his life if he chose to take it. Here was the means to get him away from this town. His life, previously miserable, would be even more so. Suddenly he knew he must leave Baptist's Hollow and never return.

Picking up the sack, Elwin stepped from the sidewalk towards his destiny. "I got your supplies here, mister. Can you take me along as far as Fort Owen?"

"Hold hard!" Haslett yelped, seeing the sack lifted into the wagon. "Is all that stuff paid for?"

"Paid for and the money in the drawer," Elwin replied. "Go and count it if you want. You can keep my week's pay."

Haslett was torn between a desire to go into his store and count the money and wishing to warn Elwin off. The latter won, and he tried to sound big as he said, "Don't you come running back here. That's the last time I take anybody in. Ungrateful bums, that's all young uns like him are."

Ellwood watched the young man climb in through the door at the rear of the wagon. Then he turned to Thornett and gave a grim warning:

"All right. Get going as soon as we know the supplies

are paid for. I want you out of this town and don't ever come back."

"Mister, do you know what you're doing?"

The soft-drawled words cut over the noise of the crowd and brought every eye to the four riders. It was the small man who'd spoken, Ellwood guessed and decided he was relying on the backing of the three big cowhands while speaking.

"What do you mean?" Ellwood asked, irritation thinly veiled in his tone. This town saw little of cowhands, less of *Texas* cowhands. Any man who knew the cowhand country would have known that here sat three men who were top-hands and knew the cattle business from calf-down to trailend shipping pens. He'd also have known that here were four men more than just ordinarily competent with their guns. Ellwood knew none of this.

"You aren't sending these folks out of town at a time like this, are you?" asked the small man.

It was Mrs. Haslett who replied, spitting the words out viciously. "Why not, because four saddle-tramps don't like it?"

"No, ma'am," the small Texan answered, his voice an easy southern drawl. "Because of what we know— and you don't."

Ellwood watched the small man, noting the commanding way in which he spoke. There was more to this man than first met the eye, the marshal decided. It might be well to listen to him.

"What might that be?"

"We found a couple of miners as we cut through the hills."

"So what?" Ellwood snapped. "The hills are full of miners."

"There's two less now, mister," the dark-faced boy said, moving his horse alongside the small man's. "Maybe more, we didn't stop on long enough to find out." He reached back and drew something from under the bedroll strapped to his saddle. "This's what killed one of them."

The crowd scattered as if the young man had thrown a live rattler at them. Every eye went to the thing which stuck in the ground before them. It looked like a long thin, straight stick—except that stick never grew on a tree with feathers at one end, barbed head at the other and painted bands of color in the center.

"But that's an Apache arrow."

"Yeah, friend," agreed the dark boy, his voice cold and mocking. "An Apache *war* arrow."

The listeners noticed the emphasis placed on that one word and knew what the dark boy meant by it. There was a whole lot the good citizens of Baptist's Hollow did not know about Apaches. There was one thing they, and almost every other man or woman in Arizona territory knew, that was the significance of an Apache war arrow. The Apache might kill a chance-met stranger with a hunting arrow, but he would never use the same for serious business. When the Apache went to war he took his special war arrows from the medicine lodge. When he used war arrows it meant just that—he was wearing paint and at war.

"So you found two dead miners, one killed by an Indian arrow," said Ellwood, not liking the dark boy's attitude or tone of voice. "Why should that stop me turning undesirables out of town?"

The small man studied Ellwood as if the marshal was fresh come from under a rotten log. "Mister, Lon said maybe more. We didn't stay on to try and find out. The Apaches are out, swarming. There's more of them out there than a man could count on a lot more hands and feet than he's got right now."

"And they're all wearing paint," concluded the dark boy, "or I don't know sic 'em about Apaches."

That was one saying none of the crowd needed explaining. No self-respecting Apache would think of making war without putting his paint on first. On the wagon Phyllis and Doc looked at the small Texan with considerable interest. They were nearly sure they could put a brand on him. It was a famous name, one which was known from Texas to California, from the Rio Grande to the Canadian line. Phyllis was almost sure but did not speak.

"That doesn't concern us any," Ellwood growled and heard his town give their rumbled agreement. "We've never had any trouble with the Apaches."

"You're like to get it," said the blond giant, his voice a deep, cultured Texas drawl. "Dusty wasn't fooling and Lon knows Indians. It'd be downright murder to send folks out there until you know the way things lay."

"We never asked them to come here in the first place," screamed Mrs. Haslett, seeing her chance to get back at Phyllis and the girls, even if it meant sending them to certain death. She hoped the show people would beg to be allowed to stay. "This's our town and we don't want the likes of them here."

The small Texan looked hard at Ellwood. "That your word?"

"Not exactly," replied Ellwood. He might have acted differently but hated the thought of being forced into a decision. "It's true we don't want their kind here, but we've seen no sign of Apaches."

The small man's eyes never left Ellwood's face. They were grey eyes, cold and hard now, the cold grey stare making the marshal feel uncomfortable. "You're sending white women out of here at a time like this. Into what could be death, or worse. When I pass the word of what you've done folks won't even spit on you in the street."

"And who'll bother to listen to the likes of you?" Mrs. Haslett sneered, her eyes studying the insignificant young Texan.

The blond youngster moved his big paint to flank his friends and spoke for the first time:

"Ma'am, I reckon folks just might listen. This here's Dusty Fog."

"Dusty Fog?" Ellwood breathed the two words out, staring at the small Texan and half suspecting a joke. "I've heard of you."

On the wagon Phyllis nudged Thornett in the ribs and smiled. Her guess was a meat-in-the-pot hit. She'd hardly recognized Dusty, for the last time she saw him was in Gratton, Texas. Then Dusty was wearing town clothes and acting as a school-teacher to help break a ruthless town-boss. The range clothes prevented Phyllis from recognizing Dusty before. She knew he recognized her by the smile he gave her before looking back at Ellwood.

The crowd knew the name. Every man here had heard of the Rio Hondo gun-wizard, Dusty Fog. His was a name to conjure with throughout the West. Dusty Fog, a small man who stood head and shoulders over the tall men he rode with. A Confederate Army captain at seventeen, Dusty built a reputation which equaled the Dixie masters, John Singleton Mosby and Turner Ashby. Since the war he'd become known as trailhand of the first water, cowhand, rough-string rider and trail boss. He was the man who brought law to the rough towns where other men failed. That was Dusty Fog, segundo of the mighty O.D. Connected ranch, nephew of the owner. Ole Devil Hardin. He was the leader of the elite of the O.D. Connected ranch crew, Ole Devil's floating outfit. Three members of the floating outfit rode with him now.

It didn't take a whole lot of brain power to guess who the three men were.

The blond giant was Mark Counter. He was a cowhand with a name as high as any man's. His father owned the biggest ranch in the Big Bend country but Mark rode as a hand with his friends. In Bushrod Sheldon's Confederate Cavalry, Mark was known as the man who set the fashion in uniforms. Now he was the Beau Brummel of the cow fighting men in the West. His skill with his fists was told of along the cattle trails; he was known to be a good rifle shot. For all of that there were few who knew of his skill with his matched guns. Those who knew said Mark Counter was second only to Dusty Fog himself in speed of draw and skill at placing home his shots.

The dark boy on the big white horse was also known —and how he was known. The Ysabel Kid was known as a rifle shot who could make a hit any time a hit was possible and frequently made a hit when a hit was impossible. He was said to be the greatest exponent of the art of cut and slash since James Bowie died at the Alamo. He was also fair with his old Dragoon gun, proving that Colonel Sam's old four-pound heavyweight was a precision weapon in skilled hands. He was spoken of as a man skilled in the noble art of reading sign. His tenor voice was much sought after by quartet singers. He could speak fluent Spanish and was conversant with six Indian tongues. His father had been an Irish Kentuckian and his mother a French Creole Comanche woman. From this mixture of bloods came a soft-talking, innocent-looking but deadly dangerous child christened Loncey Dalton Ysabel, but was better known as the Ysabel Kid.

The last member of the quartet, the handsome boy on the big paint, was known by only one name, Waco. He'd been left an orphan almost from birth by a Waco Indian attack, and from the age of thirteen was riding the cattle ranges with a low-tied gun by his side. He'd grown fast, sullen, truculent and trouble-hunting. A man who rode for Clay Allison was likely to be a real good man with a gun, and Waco was no exception to the rule. He'd ridden for the old Washita curly wolf's C.A. outfit, and with them Waco learned to handle a brace of low-tied guns. Then he met Dusty Fog and his life changed. From the day when Dusty Fog pulled Waco from in front of the stampeding C.A. herd, the youngster started to change. He'd left Allison and joined the O.D. Connected's floating outfit, changing from a proddy, trouble-hunting feller to a likeable, friendly and efficient young man. He was now known as an expert cowhand, liked and respected. To the other members of the floating outfit he gave a loyalty, brotherly respect and accepted all they could teach him. To Dusty Fog, Waco gave the devotion and hero-worship which should have gone to his father. To speak with disrespect about the Rio Hondo gun-wizard in Waco's presence was to invite a fight and to get one.

Phyllis watched the faces of the crowd, then turned to

Dusty Fog and smiled. The recognition was mutual.
Dusty knew who she was and remembered her from
their last meeting. She gave the crowd a withering glance
and said:

"We're going, Captain Fog. We wouldn't stay here if
they begged us."

For all her apparent calm Phyllis was worried. She'd
helped fight off two Indian attacks but only against
Pawnees or Utes, low down on the dangerous Indian
scale. The Apaches were right up there on top of that
scale, one of the most savage, ruthless, battle-wise and
deadly of all the fighting, Indian tribes. For all that,
even should the Apaches be waiting a mile from town,
should the death of herself and her family be certain,
Phyllis did not aim to stay in Baptist's Hollow. The very
people of the town sickened her.

"That's right," Mrs. Haslett let out a squeal. She was
disappointed that Phyllis was not begging to be allowed
to stay. "Get out of here and take your four hired killers
with you."

Dusty Fog stopped Waco's angry retort and looked
hard at Ellwood. "You know these ladies could get
killed, or worse, taken by the Apaches?"

"We've never had any Apache trouble," answered
Ellwood, worried far more than he was showing.
"Chief Ramon's a friend of our town and attends our
church. He would never allow his men to attack us."

"You sure of that?" asked the Ysabel Kid, leaning
forward slightly and looking attentive. "I mean, about
him being such a good friend?"

"He's our friend."

"Mister, you got a real dead friend," the Kid's drawl
was Comanche, deep and mean. "A fortnight back a

troop of Yankee cavalry hit his camp by mistake. They went right straight through and left poor ole Ramon dead as a six-day stunk-up skunk. Now a real bad hat, white-hater called Lobo Colorado's riding as war chief and he don't like white-eyes one lil bit.''

Ellwood stiffened and stared at the Ysabel Kid. The marshal knew something about Ramon's braves and more than somewhat about the one called Lobo Colorado. The Ysabel kid only half called it when he said Lobo Colorado was a white-hater. The Indian hated every white-skinned man, woman and child, hated them bitterly for taking away his land. With him riding as war chief it was going to mean bad trouble for the white people of Arizona. Ellwood turned to the wagon and spoke in a grudging tone:

"You can stay on here until we hear something definite. But you've got to behave and you don't try to give your show.''

"Thanks for nothing,'' snapped Phyllis, taking a chance on what she knew of the four Texans. "I wouldn't stay in your town if I knew my girls were all going to be taken alive by the Apaches. I'd prefer them to you. Come on, Doc, start the wagon.''

"You got company, happen you don't mind, ma'am,'' said Mark Counter, making the remark Phyllis guessed he would.

"Be pleased to have you along,'' Phyllis replied, trying to hide her relief. With those four along they stood a better than fair chance of getting through to Fort Owen. She looked back into the wagon where Elwin was seated and talking to her daughter. "You hear what was said, boy?''

Elwin gave a startled jump and turned to the woman. "Yes'm,'' he lied, for he'd been so engrossed talking to

Janice that he had not heard a word.

"Do you want to stay here instead of risking the fort?"

"No, ma'am!" replied Elwin in a determined voice. What Janice just told him would have made him willing to face the devil. "I'll take my chance along with you."

"Right, come on up front here while Janice changes out of that torn dress."

Ellwood was doing some right smart, fast thinking now. If Ramon was dead and Lobo Colorado rode as war chief a man could do worse than have four men like these fighting alongside him. In the war Ellwood learned the lesson of what a few good fighting men could do for an otherwise weak command. He knew the fighting qualities of his people, or the lack of fighting qualities. The four Texans might stiffen the citizens, give them hope if not courage. He made a decision which might make him unpopular with the people of the town.

"You can stay on here if you like."

"Not us, mister," replied Mark. "We wouldn't pollute your fair city no more. We'll let Fort Owen know how you're getting on."

Thornett started the wagon rolling along Church Street, headed for the stage trail. Three of the four Texans moved their horses to one side, then followed the wagon, but the fourth remained. The Ysabel Kid sat his big white, his face dark and Comanche-looking, his red-hazel colored eyes mocking and hard. For a full minute he did not speak, then he gave forth with some of his inborn Indian savvy.

"Mister, happen you've got the sense of a seam-squirrel, you'll sleep real easy tonight and every other night until Lobo Colorado's put under—— You being such a good friend of Ole Ramon, that is."

Ellwood hated the mocking note in the voice and at any other time would have reacted differently. Right now there was too much he wanted to know about Apaches, and there was not much time to learn it. Holding down his annoyance he asked:

"What do you mean?"

"Man say I know a mite about Apaches, just a lil mite," the mocking note was still there, biting and savage. "They think real funny, Apaches do. Right now, and ever since the blue-bellies put Ramon under, ole Lobo Colorado's been sending out the word for every bronco bad-hat to meet up with him, and see how little he cares for Ramon's ways and——" There was a pause, pregnant with the thought for the listening crowd. "Ramon's friends."

Ellwood was beginning to catch the drift of Ysabel's remarks and did not like what he read in them. "Well?" he asked.

"Waal, a smart ole Yankee major like you ought to be able to figure it out real good, if a half-bright lil Texas boy like me can," drawled the Kid, confirming Ellwood's suspicions. "Yeah, he'll be here one of these dawns. Him and every white-hating buck who ride hoss, or tote gun. They'll be all here, wild and r'aring to show how much they hate Ramon and his *amigos*. Mister, one morning, real early, you're going to find yourself plump belly deep in Apaches. Good luck, you'll likely wind up needing it."

With that the Ysabel Kid began to knee his big white horse around to follow his friends. Before the horse took two walking steps, Ellwood called out, "Hold it there, young man."

In all the West, as Ellwood knew from what he'd

heard, there were probably not more than two men who owned sufficient knowledge to outweigh the Ysabel Kid's "lil mite" of Indian savvy. Anything the Kid might feel like telling right now was going to be of great help to the town in preparing for the forthcoming Indian attack.

"Something bothering you, mister?" asked the Kid, turning his horse once more and bringing it to a halt.

"What'd you say was the best thing we could do?"

The Ysabel Kid looked first at the Apache war arrow which still stuck in the dirt of the street. Then slowly his eyes lifted to the scared faces of the crowd. There was quite a change in the faces now. The truculent, righteous looks were all gone, the hatred and anger faded. Only raw fear remained. The Kid looked at the people of Baptist's Hollow and his face showed what he thought of them.

"Ain't but three things you could do now. Run. But there isn't time, traveling slow like you'd be. They'd get you out in their own country—it wouldn't be pretty. You could stock that ole church there with food, powder, ball and everything. Even so, with a bunch like this to back you I wouldn't like your chances," the Kid replied, starting to turn his horse again. "Way I see it, we're lucky to be getting out of here."

"You said three things we could do, cowboy," said Ellwood in a hoarse voice. Suddenly he saw himself and his town the way this cowhand and every other person must see it. The feeling hurt, for he saw himself as a fool, a stupid, bigoted fool. Not only he himself, but almost every man and woman in the town. Now, unless they were lucky they would all wind up being dead fools. "You said three things we could do," he repeated. "What was the last thing?"

The big stallion was walking away and the Ysabel Kid did not stop it. He turned in the saddle and looked back, then replied:

"Mister, your bunch are so strong for religion and doing everything right—You might try and pray."

CHAPTER FOUR

Major Ellwood Makes Ready

Major Ellwood, town marshal of Baptist's Hollow, watched the wagon leaving his town, the four young Texas men riding behind it. He watched the four men's departure with some misgivings. If the Apaches did attack he could have used such men to back him and help in the defense of the town. They would have been just what he needed, for fighting men were desperately short in Baptist's Hollow and there were none in whom Ellwood could put his trust. Certainly not men like Haslett, Millet or the town's minister, Deacon Routh. None of them could be termed a fighting man.

The men of Baptist's Hollow stood in a group, talking among themselves about what they'd heard. Ellwood watched their faces, reading the fear in most of them. Millet was in the center of things as usual. He was a flabby fat man with a mean, piggy face which worked into folds and lines as he stressed some point. By Millet's side stood Haslett, his thin, sallow face paler than was usual as he tried to peer through the store window and see what Elwin stole when he left. Yet the thin man was so scared of missing anything that not even his mistrust of others and love of money could make him

43

leave the street. Deacon Routh, the minister, was also there, his thin, miserable face strained and scared as he tried to think up a suitable Bible quotation to cover the situation.

"What're we going to do, Major?" Haslett asked.

There Ellwood was stumped for a moment. He did not know right off just what they were going to do. Ellwood was the sort of man who needed time to think, he did not have the quick brain, the lightning speed of adaptability, which went to make a great lawman or soldier. Given a plan ready-made he could carry it out so long as it went as planned. He lacked the ability to improvise on the spot when things went wrong. His eyes went to the old Spanish church across the plaza and he remembered the Ysabel Kid's advice. There was everything to be said for their going into the church, for he knew how ideal it was for defense and protection. It would take artillery and a regiment of skilled men to break into their church if the defenders held firm. With the church supplied with food, ammunition and the necessities of life, it could be held indefinitely by determined men. Long before the Apaches could break through the defense relief would be on hand from Fort Owen. The Texans would take word to the fort, that was certain, and the cavalry could come fast.

"We'd best do what that young feller told us, fort up the church."

"I think we should assemble the Town Council and talk things out first," replied Deacon Routh. He was a shrewd judge of character and knew exactly what Haslett meant. While the good deacon did not object to any man making a profit, he did not want the same profit made at his expense.

Ellwood snorted. At this moment there was nothing

he wanted less than a meeting with the Town Council, which consisted of himself, Routh, Millet and Haslett. The purpose this council served, as Ellwood was bitterly aware, was to make sure that things ran smoothly for the members. There was no way he could avoid the meeting, so he gave his assent and turned to walk off in the direction of the jail. Millet bent to pull the Apache war arrow from the ground, then followed the other members of the council along the sidewalk.

The Town Offices of Baptist's Hollow were neither large, nor grand. They were in fact half the jail house, the other half being the steel barred cells. So little business was ever done in the office that the prisoners, if any were in the cells, could look in on any meeting. The offices themselves were nothing more than a filing cabinet in one corner and a small desk.

The two prisoners looked up as the double doors opened. Scully was clearly on his dignity as became a man who'd been jailed in most of the big towns of the West. "I say, my good man," he greeted, as Ellwood came in. "When do we eat in this pokey?"

Ellwood ignored the man and waved the council inside. Haslett was quick at counting and saw there would not be sufficient chairs to go around, so he made a dash for one, beating Routh to it by a short head. Millet laid the arrow on the desk and showed his annoyance at failing to get a seat. The arrow was an interesting object, and he might be able to sell it in his store. Then he opened the meeting with a statement worthy of his mighty brain.

"I don't think there is any Apache trouble at all. Those four brought this with them and used it as an excuse to get the show out of town."

"Why'd they bother?" asked Ellwood, wondering

how the man ever reached such a conclusion.

"They were working in with the man who ran the show. You know what those hired killers are."

Ellwood snorted, wondering where Millet kept his brains. "Why'd they need to lie about it. If they'd wanted to take the show out of town we couldn't have stopped them doing it."

Millet puffed up pompously. "I wouldn't say that, Major. I'm no man to cross when I'm roused."

Deacon Routh looked at the Apache arrow, then at the rifles which were secured to the wall by a chain through their trigger-guards and locked firmly. "Gentlemen, let us assume the warning was correct, what will be our best plan?"

"We do have our duty to the citizens to consider," agreed Haslett, "but I can't see why those men would bother to warn us."

"It could have been out of Christian charity," answered Ellwood in a low tone.

The marshal was thinking of the layout of the town now and saw a possible way of defending it. He knew little about Apache's first-hand, his knowledge coming from people he'd heard talking. The Apaches were horse-Indians, fighting from the backs of their racing war-ponies. That was one thing he was almost sure about. They were horsemen with few equals, and yet not even Apaches could ride down the slopes on three sides of the town. That meant they would come in from the open end, following the trail. There was enough room on either side of the trail for a large body of men to make a combined attack. That would be the way Lobo Colorado came, the obvious way. Any half-bright shavetail out of West Point would see that in half a glance. The Apaches would strike at dawn, coming in as the first light of day came, for that was the way they fought. Ellwood knew that much and thought back to his lessons at West Point and started to make a plan. He thought he would have little trouble in dealing with a bunch of savages, without his military training. What Ellwood was forgetting was that the Apache fought against many men with far better military training—and with some success.

"What do you think, Major?" asked Deacon Routh in a tone which suggested the marshal should have thought everything out.

Ellwood drew in a deep breath, then gave out with his plan for defending the town. "We'll dig rifle pits across the mouth of the hollow and keep them fully defended all night."

"Rifle pits?" Haslett asked, a puzzled look on his face.

"Yes, we used them in the war. Dig them just deep enough so a man can fire a rifle from them without showing too much of himself. That way he doesn't stand so much chance of getting hit. We can hold the Apaches out of town from them."

"How about the slopes on the other sides?" Haslett inquired.

"Everybody knows Apaches fight on horseback," snorted Millet, giving Ellwood his support as a way of avoiding moving his stock. "They can't ride horses down the slopes, so they won't come in that way."

"That's what I thought, too," agreed Ellwood. "Then we'll get *every* man in town to start digging out there."

Millet coughed. He was never the sort of man to relish doing any work, much less if he wasn't getting paid good hard cash for doing it. "My wife was hurt by that little hussy," he began. "I should stay by her——"

"I said every man of us," snapped Ellwood grimly. "The Town Council's going to set an example to the others. There is an election coming off soon."

"And Elvira's being well cared for by the other ladies," went on Haslett. He put his spoke in because he could not think of any excuse to avoid digging himself and did not mean that Millet should. "She'll be all right, and she'll be a whole lot worse hurt if the Apaches get in."

Millet looked around for some excuse to avoid being taken along. His eyes went to the two men in the cells. "We could make the prisoners do all the digging."

In the cells Scully gulped as he heard the words. There was one thing which he'd never committed in his life —work. He was proud of his record of never having worked any harder than toting a deck of cards up his sleeve and would die rather than get such a blemish on his spotless record. His noble sentiment was not put to the crucial test for Ellwood shook his head.

"Two men couldn't do all that digging and they'd be more trouble than they were worth if we took them along," he said. "Besides, they're only in jail pending trial, and they could sue the town if they were forced into any kind of punishment before they were tried." He paused and there was a grim set to his face. "You go out and gather all the folks, Deacon. I'm not sure we shouldn't take all your arms and ammunition to the church ready, Fred."

"There's no need for that yet," Millet answered hastily. He thought he might lose some of his goods if he let other people handle them. His greed was such that, even in this present time of danger, he would not risk losing anything. "I think we ought to get the men out and digging."

"The town should take over your food and get it up to the church ready, Haslett," Ellwood went on, looking for more support. "Just in case."

"That won't be necessary with the rifle pits dug," Haslett gulped, seeing his chance of a profit slipping. The other members of the council would not object to his making a profit—but not at their expense. They would not agree to paying more than the wholesale price if they purchased the goods from town funds.

"Go and get the men together then," Ellwood ordered and the other three men left the room. Turning to his prisoners Ellwood went on, "I'll get you a meal before I go out."

"There's no rush, Marshal," replied Scully, so grateful at not being forced to commit work that he was almost willing to forgive Ellwood for not accepting his bribe. "And thank you, sir, thank you."

Ellwood could not decide what the prisoner was thanking him for and left without inquiring. Scully and Willy exchanged glances, then both went to lay back on the hard, uncomfortable beds, ignoring the discomfort.

"That was close," said Scully.

"What's it all about?" Willy inquired. "I saw ole Doc and Miz Phyllis leave town with four men."

"Were they people from the town?" asked Scully, for he liked Doc and Phyllis.

"Nope, they wus cowhands and good uns at that."

"There was some talk of Apaches," Scully mused, looking up at the room. "I wouldn't want to be caught in here by Apaches. It wouldn't be restful or pleasant."

Ellwood found a sullen, mutinous crowd awaiting

him outside the office. The citizens of the town had one thing in common, a dislike for doing anything which did not pay a return in good, hard cash. They were so narrow-minded that none could see the sense in digging holes which might never be needed. There was still less enthusiasm when they realized they'd be forced to man the same holes.

One of the men stepped forward. "Look here, Major," he said truculently. "We been talking things over and we don't reckon there's any need for us to get all hot and bothered. Maybe a couple of miners were killed in the hills, maybe there wasn't. We ain't but got the words of them four men for it. Even if they did find the two miners it don't mean Ramon's people done it. It could have been done by renegades. Anyways, we haven't heard from the Army yet."

Ellwood was beginning to hate the people of his town, hate their selfish ways and actions. "So?" he asked grimly.

"The stage comes in at noon today."

"I know that."

"Last one come in a week back."

"What're you getting at?"

"It won't be running if the Apaches are out, now will it?"

"It wouldn't, most likely," agreed Ellwood. "If folks knew about the Apaches being out, that is."

"Then how about waiting until one o'clock?" the man demanded.

There was some sense in what the man was saying. Ellwood conceded the point, for he knew that the Wells Fargo Company would not be running their stage if they knew of Apache trouble. This was also a slack time of the year, and only one coach could be guaranteed to run. That was the fast mail carrying coach to Fort Owen, it was due in Baptist's Hollow at noon this day, and the driver was proud of his boast that he was never late. The only trouble with waiting was that it would have wasted valuable time which could profitably be spent in preparing the defenses of the town. Ellwood knew there was no chance of getting anything done by his people until they were sure it was absolutely necessary, so he gave in with bad grace.

"All right, do what you want," he snapped. "But if that coach isn't here by one o'clock, we're starting to dig those pits without any more talk."

The crowd dispersed and Ellwood went back to the jail. He was in a mood and did no more than grunt in reply to Scully's questions. There was no reason why the Texans should lie to him. They were not working with the medicine show. He'd heard enough of Dusty Fog and the others to know they never sold their guns. Even if they were working in with the show there would have been no need to lie. There was no man, or bunch of men, in Baptist's Hollow, who could have stopped the forceable leaving of the show. That was an Apache war arrow the Ysabel Kid threw at the feet of the crowd, and Ellwood was fully aware of the significance of such a weapon.

It was then Ellwood remembered that Chief Ramon and the other few converted Apaches were not at church for the past two Sundays. The chief was usually one of the best attenders to church, yet he suddenly stopped coming. Ellwood had always been suspicious of Ramon's motives in becoming a Christian and expected him to give it up when he found he could make nothing out of it. Now Ellwood wondered. He would not have thought anything about the Apache's non-arrival. Now

he was not so sure, he felt something had gone wrong.
The feeling grew on him as the minutes ticked away,
dragging on towards one o'clock.

Noon came and went without a sign of the stage. Only
a few men were on the street at noon, for all of them expected the familiar sight of the coach lumbering at full
speed along the street, making a turn in the plaza and
coming to a halt before the Wells Fargo office. At ten
past one there were worried looks and a few more of the
citizens began to gather. By twenty past the worried
looks were getting more and more in evidence. Then
Millet gave an excited yell and pointed off towards the
stage trail.

"Something's coming! Look at that dust!"

Ellwood looked in the direction of the pointing finger
and saw dust, but not enough for the stage-coach to be
making it. The others were watching the dust without
giving any thought to how much or little there was. A
few malicious grins were directed at Ellwood, and the
men were ready to mock their marshal for having been
taken in and fooled by the four Texans.

The grins faded from the faces as one riderless horse
came into sight, turned from the range trail and headed
down to the town on the run. A horse without a saddle,
but with broken harness trailing behind it. The horse
was flecked with sweat, the ears were laid back and the
eyes rolled in panic as it ran. Ellwood was the first to
react. He leapt forward and caught the horse's trailing
reins, bringing it to a stop. Talk welled up from the
crowd, excited and frightened talk as they looked at the
big bay horse. Even without the stage-line's brand on
the hip, everyone in the crowd knew where it came
from. They saw the raw, bloody furrow on the side and
all could guess at the cause of it.

There were no grins now, no thoughts of mocking their marshal for being a fool. The coach would not be coming, that was obvious. It would be out there on the trail some place, wrecked, the driver, guard and passengers either dead, or wishing they were. This one horse must have broken free, driven wild by panic and started to run. It must have followed the trail and turned down to the town through instinct, doing as it always did when hauling the stage.

"I reckon we'd best get those rifle pits dug now," Ellwood snapped, and for once there was no argument to his orders.

Never did the citizens of Baptist's Hollow throw themselves into a task with no personal gain as they did right now. They worked with the speed that only fear could inspire. Hands long unused to doing heavy work swung picks, shovels and crowbars with vigor, if not skill, sinking the pits as deep as the rock would allow. It was not as deep as Ellwood would have liked, but there was no other way to make them deeper. Not without blasting powder, and Ellwood did not wish to take time out to blast the holes. He climbed into one and found that by kneeling a man would be able to fire his rifle and still find safety. Ellwood was satisfied with the finished result. Knowing his people he'd never hoped to get so much done. In that he did the citizens of Baptist's Hollow an injustice. They knew their lives were in danger and were willing to work hard at anything which would save them.

A man suddenly dropped his shovel and gave a startled yell, pointing off towards the hills. "Look up there!" he yelled.

The others looked and panic filled them. Dust was rolling up in the hills, a moving cloud and coming their way, beneath the dust could be seen vague shapes of riding men. It was at that moment the working party realized how few of their number were armed.

Millet, as befitting a leading member of the community, gave an example of how to act in such an emergency. Dropping his shovel he gave a howl of:

"Run for it. Apaches!"

Ellwood was watching the dust and he snapped, "Apaches, nothing. They're miners from the hills."

"Miners?" asked Millet, scowling, then raising his hand to peer at the figures from under its shade. "So they are. I've not got me spectacles with me, or I'd have seen that afore."

For all that Millet licked his lips and looked ready to bolt. The figures were closer now, and he could make out that they were definitely not Indians. He recognized most of the riders, but this was the first time he'd ever seen so many of them coming into town at one time.

Seventeen men rode slowly towards the town, traveling in a loose group. Tall, lean, grizzled and bearded men wearing buckskins and riding shaggy Indian ponies. Each of this pair nursed a Remington Rolling Block rifle across his knees and belted a revolver. Every other man in the group was armed, rifle out and ready, revolver holstered at his side. They made a hard-looking bunch, fighting men all of them, and men who knew the Arizona country. They were worried men also. That showed in the wolf-cautious way they rode and watched the surrounding country.

Ellwood watched the approaching party. He knew all of them and most had been in his jail for drunkenness at one time or another. The two old-timers in front and the short, broad oldster, riding a mule and leading a burro, at the rear, were always cautious. There was more than just plain caution right now.

The miners came nearer without changing their pace any. The two men in the lead brought their horses to a halt. The taller looked down at the pits, spat out a well-chewed wad of tobacco and asked:

"You heard something, Major?"

"What about?" asked Ellwood.

"The Apaches done put their paint on. That's why me'n ole Ike here cut out and found the other boys," the miner said, indicating his partner. "War a few we couldn't find. Found one family and buried what was left. So we didn't take no more time out to find the others—what's left of 'em."

"Have you seen any Apaches?" Millet asked worriedly. These men were all well-versed in Apache ways, and their testimony was more to be believed than the words of a bunch of Texas cowhands.

"Plenty in our time, me'n Zeke have," the man called Ike answered. "War seeing 'em real regular until two-three days back."

"Then we stopped seeing 'em," went on Zeke grimly. "So we concluded to git up and the hell out of the Dragoons for a piece. Us and all them as could."

The other miners gave a grunting agreement to the words. They knew Apaches and knew full well when it was time to yell "calf-rope" and head for a safer area than their small mining claims in the Dragoon Mountains. Any white man still in the Dragoons would likely be staying there permanently.

"What do you mean?" asked Haslett, looking nervously around and imagining Apaches behind every bush. "You come in when you *stopped* seeing Apaches?"

Zeke took his attention from the rifle pits and looked at the scared face of the storekeeper. "Waal, I ain't eddicated, but there's one lil thing I allus did l'arn. When you sees Apaches everything's all right and peace falls full 'n' rich on the land. When you stops seeing 'em it's full gone time to start and worry—And mister, we done stopped seeing 'em.''

''So you just left your claims and walked out?'' Millet inquired.

''No friend,'' replied Zeke, sun-squinted eyes on the fat man. ''We didn't walk at all—we ran.''

''You'll excuse me iggerance, Major,' put in Ike, before the spluttering Millet could say another word. He indicated the rifle pits with a contemptuous wave of his hand. 'Jest what do ye brand them things with?''

''They're rifle pits,'' Haslett pompously explained.

''Now me,'' grunted Zeke. ''I figgered you'd started in to dig for gold. You fixing in to fight Apaches from them things?''

''What else would you have us do?'' Ellwood growled. It was a pity that his nerves were jumpy, and his tone held such a note. He really wanted help from these men, but his tone was sharp and forbidding.

''Nothing, Major. Nothing at all,'' Ike replied mildly. ''Allow you all knows what you're doing.''

''Of course he does,'' barked Millet, annoyed that these uneducated miners were trying to interfere. ''The Major fought in the Civil War.''

''Saloon open yet?'' drawled Zeke, interrupting Millet's speech.

The saloon-keeper dropped his pick and rubbed his hands on his trousers. ''It can be, if you want something.''

''Hold hard there,'' Millet snapped as the saloon-keeper turned to head for the town. ''We don't want men traipsing off——''

"Wants us some powder, lead and hulls, too," Ike interrupted.

Millet's good intentions faded off right away. He swung his shovel over his shoulder and headed for town. The other men watched Millet and the saloon-keeper and prepared to leave. Ellwood allowed the miners to ride by, then called the citizens back. They came slowly and reluctantly, facing him.

"I want these pits manning all night. We'll split the town into two groups."

"Can't the miners do it?" asked Haslett. "They're stopping in *our* town and they ought to take on the defense of it. You could bring them here and——"

"I said all of you would take it in turns," Ellwood cut in, his voice cold, grim and determined. "I'll see the miners and ask them if they'll take a turn, but we can't force them to. I think that the Town Council should take the last turn, just to set the others a good example."

There was a lot of agreement to this, although the members of the council were not among those who agreed. For once the council was voted under and Haslett went off with Deacon Routh muttering to themselves, threatening to get a new town marshal elected as soon as this trouble was over.

Ellwood followed the digging party back to town, satisfied with what he'd done so far towards the safety of the people. The arrival of the miners was a blessing, for they confirmed that the Apache were out. They were also a most useful addition to his fighting strength and if they would help man the pits might hold the Apaches out of town.

The miners reached town and left their horses in the livery barn. The short old-timer called Walapai kept his burro with him. He never went anywhere without his old Winnie-Mae at his heels. He and the burro were just about inseparable, he even took it into the saloon with him. Winnie-Mae could put away a fair amount of beer, although she never developed a taste for whisky.

Heading for Haslett's place first the miners stocked themselves with food. It was unfortunate that Haslett was not there, for his wife sold at the normal price instead of shoving the value up. With their food, they headed for Millet's store and found him there waiting for them. Millet was no hero, and there was a look in the grim eyes of the miners which warned him not to try and make a sudden profit out of them. He went down into the cellar, through the trapdoor behind the counter and brought up powder from the big barrel where he stored it. The miners bought their supplies of ammunition, powder and lead, then made for the saloon. Zeke stopped at the door of the store and looked at the shelves, the rifles in the rack, the pistols of various kinds in the display counter.

"What you fixing in to do with all this lot, Millet?" he asked. "Might be as well to get it down to the old church there, ready for them when the attack comes."

"It might be," agreed Millet cautiously.

"Me'n the boys'll bear a hand to tote it down," Zeke offered, and to do him justice he had no ulterior motive in the offer.

"There's no need for you to bother," Millet replied hastily, sure the miner was only offering so as to rob him. "I've got it all arranged."

"Nice to know," grunted Zeke and left the building.

Ellwood knew where to find the miners when he came to town. He looked at the sun as it sank in the west, reddening the sky. They'd wasted so much time and it would be dark before he could think of starting to move the arms from Millet's place to the church. The miners would be a big help to him now. They would form the mainstay of his defense.

Pushing open the saloon doors Ellwood stepped inside, looking at the miners. They were seated in small groups, silently nursing glasses of beer. He could see very little drinking was being done and this surprised him. For a miner out of the hills, a trip to town usually meant a prolonged drinking spree. His eyes went to old Walapai, who sat with his moccasined feet on the table top, then to the burro as it sank its nose into a bucket filled with beer. None of the miners spoke and at last Ellwood asked:

"How many of you'll come out to the rifle pits after dark?"

There was no reply to this, the miners carrying on with their quiet drinking. Finally Zeke put down his glass, spat into the spittoon and came to his feet.

"You want some advice, Major?"

Ellwood did want advice. Needed it badly. But his cross-grained nature would not allow him to accept it. "I want to know if you're willing to fight under my orders. That's all," he snapped back. "How about it?"

"Sorry, Major," Walapai spoke up. "I get screwmatics bad. Couldn't stand in a hole all night."

"They allows the dawn air's real bad in one of them things, comes to that," Ike drawled. "Deal me out."

"I might have expected that," Ellwood barked, although the very refusal ought to have warned him. "All right, finish your drinks, this place's closed. See to it, Mannering."

The saloon-keeper nodded sullenly. He was looking forward to a good and unexpected night's business and did not like the idea of having it spoiled. There was no arguing with the town marshal, not when one word would close the saloon for good. "You heard the man, boys," he said miserably. "I've got to do it."

"Finished drinking any ways," Zeke replied, watching the doors close behind Ellwood. "Damn fool. What do you reckon, Walapai?"

"I floats my stick along of you, Zeke. Should try and talk 'em into moving the powder and shot to the church. Don't reckon they will though. Ain't going to listen to no low folks like us."

"He'll get these folks killed for certain sure," Ike drawled. "Let's call us a miner's meeting down to the church and decide what we aims to do."

Whatever the thoughts and anxieties of the miners, the citizens of Baptist's Hollow felt none. They were contented that they were safe behind that line of holes in the ground. Why should they worry, they were led by a man who fought in the Civil War and learned his business under real war conditions, against white soldiers. The defense of the town could safely be left in his capable hands.

CHAPTER FIVE

Apache Ambush

"I never thought to see you out this way, Captain," Phyllis remarked to the small Texan as they left the town and turned on to the main stage trail.

"Could have knocked me down with a buffalo bull when I saw you, Miss Phyl," Dusty Fog replied, smiling. "We came out this way to pick up a bunch of blood horses from Colonel Raines, up to Backsight. Found the two miners and came into town to let them know about it. Say, Mark, this here's Madam Fiona. I told you about her. Met her in Gratton while I was handling that chore for Sam William."

Phyllis's rich smile showed her pleasure at the meeting, and the pleasure was not entirely selfish. She was pleased to have Dusty Fog's escort, but she would have been just as pleased to meet him at any time. The small Texan was something of a hero to her, even though he was the cause of her losing the only fight of her career.

"Right pleased to know you, ma'am," drawled Mark, touching his hat brim to her. "I'd surely admire to see you in action."

"And you shall, you shall," boomed Thornett delightedly. "Madam Fiona is defending her title against a challenger at Fort Owen."

"Who'd that be, ma'am?" Mark asked with some interest. He was a keen student of the art of pugilism and could have contended for top honors in the ring.

"Some girl Paddy Magoon found," Phyllis replied. She was never ashamed of her fist fighting and would talk of it any time. "I don't know who it is they've got up at Fort Owen. Last time Paddy got a two hundred pound Osage squaw."

"Magoon?" Dusty put in. "He wouldn't be a big, red-haired Irishman with a thirst that'd empty a barrel, a temper touchier than a teased rattler and more guts than you could hang on the big corral fence?"

"It sounds like you know him well," replied Phyllis, smiling. "I've only met him three times, but he proposed to me each time."

"I know him all right," Dusty agreed, also smiling. "Met him in the Black Hills country in seventy-five."

Mark studied Phyllis with some interest, for he'd heard about her. He'd seen several women bare-fist boxers, for they were as popular as girl wrestlers were later to become. He knew that while some of the girls could not punch their way through a well soaked sheet of paper, there were others who could have given a strong man a hard match. From all he'd heard of Phyllis she was one of the latter. From her appearance she looked strong and capable.

Patty, Rosie and Molly were at the front of the wagon, looking at their escort with some interest. Janice and Elwin were in the wagon, talking a blue-streak to each other, making plans. Janice was changed now, wearing a clean gingham dress and her face cleared of blood.

"Say, wasn't you the lady fist-fighter Miss Freddie wanted to get to her place in Mulrooney, Kansas, ma'am?" Waco asked, winking at Rosie.

"We arrived and the match was arranged, my boy," Thornett answered. He knew why the Texans were talking. They wanted to prevent the girls thinking of the danger they were in. They were in danger, he knew that from the way the Texans drew their saddle-guns as soon as they left the town and were nursing the Winchesters as they rode.

"Are the Apaches really out, Kid?" Molly asked, rifle in hand.

"Out and waiting, gal," answered the Kid, eyeing the rifle. "Don't you go shooting me in the leg with that thing."

"Molly'd hit anything you could, faster, neater and further off," Rosie put in, full of pride in her sister.

Molly looked down at the rifle in the Kid's hands, biting off an exclamation at what she saw. It was a magnificent weapon, the barrel rich blued and engraved by a master craftsman, the woodwork finest black walnut. It was one of the superb, "One of a Thousand," Winchester Model '79s and set into the butt was a tarnished silver plate on which she could just read the engraved words:

"Presented to Loncey Dalton Ysabel.

FIRST PRIZE, Rifle Shoot, Cochise County Fair."

There was respect in her eyes as she looked at the Indian dark boy, for Molly knew how much skill and shooting savvy was needed to win that rifle shooting match. The finest rifle-shots in the West were entered for it and this was the man who won. Nudging Rosie hard in the ribs Molly warned:

"You keep good and quiet, little sister. This's one

man I won't want to tangle with in a shooting match."

"Say Phyl," Mark said. "You all ever meet up with a German girl called Eeney Haufman?"

"Sure, that's going back a few years. She gave me a good fight. Did you know her?"

"Why sure," Mark agreed.

Dusty slowed his horse to a walk, allowing the wagon to pull ahead of him. He left Mark and Waco to talk with the girls and keep them amused, for Dusty wanted to do some fast, uninterrupted thinking. He wanted his plans made ready, in case the Apaches jumped them. He also wanted to think over the situation and call on the Kid's Indian savvy. He saw the Kid was allowing the wagon to pass and rode alongside his friend. Neither spoke for a moment, then Dusty asked:

"How do you see it, Lon?"

"Like this. Ole Ramon was a friend of the white-eyes, now he's dead. Lobo Colorado's in Ramon's place and he's going to strike out."

"You sure of that?"

"Sure as I am of salvation, or ever surer. He'll hit out with his men to show the others how he hates white-eyes."

"Then we've got to guess where he'll hit first," said Dusty. "How do you see that town back there?"

"Be a good place for him to make his move," agreed the Kid. "Man said Ramon went to their church, was their friend. That makes them the best bet for it. You can bet all you've got that Lobo Colorado's got them folks figgered out for what they are and knows for certain they'd be the easiest place to make a start. Easy kills and easy coups, plenty of loot to show the others who aren't ready for war. Yes sir, Dusty, Baptist's Hollow's the most likely place for him to hit."

For a moment Dusty thought of heading back and offering to help defend the town, but he discarded the idea. There was no guarantee Lobo Colorado would strike at the town, only a guess. The sooner the Army learned that an uprising was in the air the better. Now Dusty and his party was clear of the town there and no sense in their going back. Their best bet would be to push on to the fort and warn the Cavalry. Dusty knew that there might be trouble if he returned. He was not the sort of man to stand by and watch a job botched. If the defense of the town was not being handled correctly he would step in, and he knew the kind of people who inhabited Baptist's Hollow.

Dusty turned to his Indian-dark friend, and the Kid knew orders were coming. So did the other two Texans, and they left off talking to hear what Dusty said.

"Lon, take a point ahead. Make a sweep along the trail for the next three or four miles. Do you know this part of the world, Doc?"

"Never been out here before," Thornett answered. "Perchance our young friend in the wagon might know something."

Elwin came to the open front of the wagon, having unwillingly stopped talking to Janice. It took a minute for Dusty's question to sink in, for Elwin to think out a sensible answer. His head was full of thoughts about a pretty little girl who appeared to like him and who thought he could make a living juggling. Finally he managed to sort out a reply.

"There's a relay station about six or seven miles ahead, mister."

"Make for it, Lon," ordered Dusty. "See how the folks who run it are. If you don't come back and tell us different, we'll follow you up slow and easy like. Hold your team down to a walk, Doc. We don't want them tiring any if we have to make a run for it."

The Ysabel Kid rode ahead, allowing his huge white stallion to pick a fast, easy pace, the kind of gait the huge horse could cover miles at and still keep enough left inside for a real fast run should one become necessary. He rounded a bend in the trail and was out of sight of the wagon, thick brush closing in on either side of the trail. This was not the sort of country a man would ride through, happen he was given first pick at the remuda, but Dusty was right in having a scout out ahead.

Sliding the rifle back into the saddleboot the Kid rode on, alert and with every sense working full time. In this sort of country he would not need the extra range and magazine capacity of the Winchester. If he needed a weapon at all the shorter barrel, harder hitting power and better, easier handling qualities of the Dragoon would be called for. His rifle would only be in the way, so he shoved it back and relied on that four-pound thumb-busting giant made in Hartford sometime around 1851 which now, in his holster, was ready to prove time had not diminished its powers.

Riding scout, even in dangerous country like this, was the Ysabel Kid's favorite sport. Playing off his alert, keen, Indian-smart senses against a dangerous and deadly enemy was a good gamble. Even with his life and the lives of his friends as forfeit if he failed. At such times he was far more Indian than white, the wild Comanche blood taking control of him as he rode. His dark face was impassive and emotionless, his eyes flickering this way and that in fast, all-embracing glances which missed nothing. Beneath his legs the huge white stallion appeared to have caught the feeling of the situation, caught the tenseness in the air, it looked far more like a wild creature than a domesticated animal. Moving along almost in complete silence the huge white stallion held its head up, ears cocked to catch any slight sound and nostrils quivering to detect any wind borne scent. It looked as alert, nervous and ready as a mule-dear sneaking through a well-hunted thicket.

For three miles the Kid rode, holding his horse to the same fast lope and pulling further ahead of the wagon all the time. He did not allow this to worry him; the further ahead the better he liked it. If he ran into an ambush, there would be a better chance of his getting clear and back to allow Dusty to prepare a defense. He knew the Apache pony was not sired that could outrun the big white. If he once got clear of the ambush, they would never catch up with him.

All the time the Kid watched the trail and the bush for any sign which might give him warning. He saw nothing, but that did nothing to lull him. That was the time when the Apache was most dangerous, when he was unseen. If anything, the lack of sign made him more alert. His every instinct warned him he was being watched, and he had no cause to doubt his instincts. They seldom, if ever, failed him. Somewhere near at hand an Apache, or maybe more, was watching him.

The big white threw back its head and snorted. At the same moment the Kid heard a faint fizzing sound. He heard it as he fell sideways from the back of his horse, falling, right-hand twisting, palm out, to lift clear the old Dragoon gun.

Even as the Kid tipped sideways from the saddle there sounded a dull bellow, and he heard the slap of a close-passing bullet. The shot passed through where his body had been an instant before. It was a neat ambush, well laid and well executed. The charge of the smoothbore musket would have torn through his body, without his superb coordination of mind and muscle. A slower thinking and acting man would have resulted in one very dead white-eye.

The Ysabel Kid pitched from his saddle, and the big horse shot forward, running down the trail. This was an old and well-learned trick. The big white headed out of the possible firing area, then swung off into the brush and, once clear of the track, stood hidden and waited for further orders.

Lighting down, rolling, the Kid went under the shelter and cover of a scrub-oak by the side of the trail. He ended his roll facing the trail. Dragoon Colt cocked in his right hand, eyes glowing savagely. He was full ready to shoot, for there would be at least one Apache, maybe more, at the other side of the trail. They were awaiting for another crack at him, waiting patiently. There was no sign of them, and the Kid did not expect any sign for some time, so he settled down to wait, to allow the Apaches to make the first move.

Knowing Apaches, the Kid was ready for a long wait. They were just as patient and lay watching the place where he disappeared. The Apaches would be waiting for him to make the first move. It was the Apache way, a deadly war of nerves and death waiting for the first to make a wrong move.

Slowly, silently, an inch at a time the Kid braced his left leg under him ready to lunge forward when the Apaches showed themselves. His keen ears, working even more keenly at such a time, caught a faint scraping sound, a sound so slight that less keen ears would have overlooked or missed it completely. The Kid neither missed, nor ignored the sound, for he knew what made it. One of the braves on the other side of the trail was ramming a fresh charge down the barrel of the old flintlock smoothbore. The scraping sound was caused by the ramrod on the inside of the barrel.

All went silent again, silent as the grave. Off in the bush the Kid knew his big white stallion was standing like a statue, waiting for the whistle which would bring the horse back to him. The pitch of the whistle would tell Blackie if it must come back at a walk, or with a rush.

Nothing moved, everything deathly still. Even the birds were silent, as if they knew the deadly drama being enacted by the sides of the trail. The Ysabel Kid lay still and unmoving as a deadly black shadow, his old Dragoon gun ready to fire.

Then suddenly there were two young Apaches on the trail. They came into view in complete silence. One minute the trail was empty, the next they were on it and moving forward, towards where the Kid disappeared when he fell from his horse. One held an old flintlock mustket, the other carried a bow, arrow on string but not drawn back as yet.

Their sudden appearance almost took the Kid by surprise. They should have waited much longer before making an appearance. It was then the Kid saw how young the two were, boys fresh from horse-herding. It was all clear now, older hands would never have shown themselves that way, or come out so quickly. Come to that, older hands carried better than an old flintlock muzzle-loader which fizzed out a warning as the powder in the frizzen-pan burned before igniting the main firing charge in the barrel. These were not old hands, they were but boys on their first war trail. They were never going to make it to being battle-tried, experienced warriors. Or if they were Loncey Dalton Ysabel was slipping badly.

With eager grins the braves started forward, towards the victim who they fondly imagined lay dead. Their grins died as the same victim came lunging out from the other side of the trail. He landed half-crouched before them, his old gun swinging up to line on them. He came fast, silent and moved faster than they were capable of moving. The old Dragoon bellowed like a cannon, flame lancing from the barrel, and the brave holding the musket was flung backwards from his feet by the impact of the soft, round lead ball, powered by a full forty grain charge of prime Du Pont powder.

Through the whirling eddies of the powder smoke, the Kid saw the other Apache bring back his bowstring ready to release the arrow. The Kid was moving Indian fast, his reactions just that much ahead of the young Apache. He flung himself to one side even as he shot down the first brace, trying to get clear of the smoke, get a clear shot—and avoid the arrow. The brave was fast, his arrow cut through the Kid's vest as it swung away from his body. The Kid drew back the hammer of his old Dragoon and let it fall, strike the percussion cap and send a tiny jet of flame into the chamber below. There was a roar, and the round ball was expelled through the seven-and-a-half-inch barrel of the Dragoon.

The bow-toting brave was spun around, his left shoulder almost torn from his body by the .44 ball. Even as he went down, the brave tried to get his knife out and carry on the fight. There was no hesitation in the way the Kid acted now. The brave was an Apache, even if a young one, and as such he was dangerous as long as there was breath in his body. Lining the gun carefully, the Kid fired again and the ball tore the top of the brave's head away. The young Apache slammed back to the ground and lay there, limbs quivering.

Even as the brave was going down, the Kid went into cover again, moving faster than a greased weasel. His gun was still out and ready, and he felt sweat making his black shirt cling to his back. By all fair means he should be dead right now, either bullet or arrow sunk into his body. There should be at least one more Apache in the bushes, covering the other two. That one must have missed his chance, the Kid decided and waited for some sign.

Once more silence fell, broken only by the moaning of the wounded Apache on the trail. The Kid was still again, his palm felt sticky and his mouth was suddenly dry. He was scared and not ashamed of the fact. Any man who knew enough about Apaches would have been scared at a time like this. Fear did not make him either relax or panic, for it was sensible fear, nearer to caution than fear proper. He'd got just three loads left in his gun. There was not time to reload, even if he was able to do so. This was one of the rare times when the Kid almost wished he owned a metal cartridge firing Peacemaker, even with its comparatively light, twenty-eight grain, powder charge. If he owned a Peacemaker he would have been carrying extra bullets in his cartridge loops on the gunbelt. There was no way he could carry spare loads for his Dragoon, his powder flask and bullet bag were in his warbag. Even with the flask and bullets on hand it took time to reload the Dragoon, and time was one thing the Ysabel Kid was fresh out of.

The wounded Apache was on his knees now, not trying to get to cover as he wailed out his death song. It was at that moment the Comanche in the Kid gave him the answer to the missing Apache. The two braves who came out were just that—two, no more. If there'd been more of the same age all would have come out at the same time, and if there'd been an older brave along it would not have been the Apaches lying out on the trail.

The Ysabel Kid came out of cover again, giving a shrill whistle which brought the sound of his horse moving back towards him. Coming out of the bushes, the Kid advanced to give the Apache a merciful bullet. There was nothing could save the Apache boy now, no medical power great enough to stop his dying, even if the Kid felt like leaving him alive. The brave was done for, the .44 ball having torn right through his body. Stepping forward the Kid lined his revolver, then listened to the words the brave wailed out:

"My father is shamed! My lodge is shamed! I have failed my chief!"

At times like this the Ysabel Kid thought and acted like an Indian. There were few more chivalrous warriors than the Indian when fighting against one of his own kind. That was why the Kid spoke instead of shooting. He lowered his gun, without holstering it, then in the deep throated, guttural Apache tongue asked:

"Why so, brother?"

The young Apache looked up, agony twisting his face as he focused his eyes on the white man who fought like an Indian and spoke his own tongue so well.

"Lobo Colorado sent Antelope Boy and me to bring all brave-heart warriors to make the great medicine battle at the village of the stone god house. It is his big medicine and will show all men that Lobo Colorado is the leader who will drive the white-eyes from our land. We should have gone on and left you, but Antelope Boy saw you and said we should count coup on you. Also he wanted your big white horse, your rifle and little gun. I did not want to waste time, but he said you are only a white man and would be easy to kill," the dying youngster said. He shuddered, then stiffened himself to prevent the other man seeing any sign of pain. "Now I know you are no white-eye. What tribe do you come from?"

The Kid was not ashamed of his Indian blood and proud of the tribe to which he belonged. "I am Comanche."

"I am ashamed, Comanche," the young Apache gasped out. "My lodge is shamed, and my father will never sing my praise at the council fire, for I have failed my chief!" He coughed, the blood running down his chin. "My horse is in the bush, Comanche. If you bring it to me and help me mount, I can die a warrior's death, trying to do as my chief wants."

The Ysabel Kid did not even think of refusing the Apache's request. He turned and went into the brush and found two wiry ponies fastened to a tree. He unfastened them and led them back to the trail. The young Apache managed to get to his feet, although how he managed it the Kid could not tell. Helping the young Apache to mount the Kid stepped back and looked up. Gripping his horse's mane and clinging to its flanks with his knees, the young brave gasped out:

"Soon there will be a great battle, Comanche. Lobo Colorado has made his medicine, and the coups at the village of the stone god house will be the sign. Die well when Lobo Colorado comes."

"I'll try, brother," answered the Kid. "Die well!"

The Apache rode his horse from the trail and disappeared out of sight into the bushes, his death song com-

ing back to the Kid. Then there was a strangled gasp and
a thud, followed by the noise of the horse moving at a
better speed. The young Apache brave died happy, trying to obey the orders of his chief.

The Kid would deny that he was any kind of sen-
timentalist. He'd done what he could for his enemy,
acted as a Comanche Dog Soldier should. Now it was
long gone time to be away from here. The big white
came up, and the Kid dragged the dead Indian to one
side of the trail. Then he gripped the saddlehorn and
vaulted afork the horse with a lithe, Indian-like bound.
This would not be a healthy spot if there were other
Apaches around.

In the saddle the Kid gave some sudden thought as to
what he should do now. He should go back and warn
Dusty about the ambush and tell what he knew. He
should also go on to the relay station and warn the men
working it, if they did not already know or were still
alive to profit from the warning.

So the Kid turned his horse towards the relay station
and rode on. Dusty must be told about the attack on
Baptist's Hollow. It would most likely come at dawn.
However, the horses needed watering, and the nearest
water was at the relay station. So that was where the Kid
must head now and wait for Dusty to catch up.

The need for caution was even greater now, and the
Kid rode with care. His shots would be likely to bring
any Apaches swarming in to investigate. If there were
other and older braves in the vicinity, the slightest in-
attention would give them their chance, and he would be
aware of their presence. As aware as a man could get
with a barbed killing arrow through his body.

There was no sign of life on the ride. The Kid might
have been the only living thing in Arizona Territory. He

felt relieved when the bush opened up ahead of him, and he saw the remains of the relay station ahead. Where once stood a stout wooden shack, outbuildings and corrals, there was now nothing but charred timbers. From the lack of smoke, the Kid guessed the fire was long over. Long enough for safety at any rate.

Reaching down, he drew his rifle and rode forward. The open land was still as far as the eye could see. It rolled off into the foothills, and they rose to the heights of the Dragoon Mountains. The scenic beauty held no charm for the Kid. His attention was on that burned-out building.

Dropping from the big white, the Kid made a careful check of the building. He laid a hand on the charred timbers and found his guess was right. The fire had been over long enough for the timbers to have cooled now. There was only one more thing to do, something which must be done before the wagon brought Phyllis and her daughters to the lay station.

Making a circle of the area on foot the Kid checked over everything he could find, reading a story from the sign on the ground. With relief, he saw that the relay station people got clear before the attack. They pulled out with all their horses a week back. Shrewd men, those two, reading the signs and getting out while the going was good and safe. He wondered where they'd gone to and hoped they were lucky enough to make it. A herd of prime horses would be like a magnet to every trouble-hunting Apache.

The burning of the building happened two days after the agents pulled out. A small party, eight or so strong, came on the place looking for coups and loot. They took all they wanted and burned the rest.

The Kid took his horse to the banks of a small stream

near the station, and after removing the saddle allowed the big white to drink. Then he loaded his old Dragoon and, from his warbag, took his second weapon, another of the heavy old Dragoon guns, but of a later model. This weapon was loaded and only needed capping, so he placed on the percussion caps and sat back to wait for his friends.

CHAPTER SIX

Big Em

The medicine show wagon came into sight of the burned-out relay station. Out front, Winchester carbine resting butt down on his knee, rode Dusty Fog; his eyes flickered left and right in fast but careful looks which missed little. Mark Counter rode to the right of the wagon, also holding his rifle; Waco brought up the rear, no longer talking with Rosie, for the door was closed. He rode easily, yet his Winchester was ready for instant use, and the back trail held a fascination for him. They all showed some relief at finding their friend alive and well.

The Ysabel Kid came to his feet in a lithe bound and walked towards the approaching wagon. He glanced at Phyllis and her three daughters who were standing at her back. All of them looked pale and shaken by what they'd seen on the trail, and the Kid cursed his stupidity in leaving the Apache's body in plain view. He should have dragged the body out of sight of the trail, not just left it lying where the girls could see it.

"Man'd say you ran into a mite of trouble back there, Lon," drawled Waco as he rode forward to greet his friend. "Way I read the sign war two lots of trouble. I didn't see but one, though."

"A man can tell your work any place, you damned Comanche," growled Mark. "The way that ole cannon tears a man you can't miss the sign."

Dusty stopped his big paint and looked around the open area. His eyes met the Kid's asking a question and receiving a head shake in reply. The Kid indicated where the station agents made their escape. So Dusty made his decision. Here would be a good place to allow the horses to rest, water and graze. It was also a place which they could easily defend if need arose.

"Couple of young bucks tried to take me," answered the Kid. "Got both of them. One told me it's to be Baptist's Hollow for the first attack."

"Two of them?" Dusty inquired, watching his friend's face and reading more in it than any other living person could have. "There was only one by the side of the trail."

"Why sure," agreed the Kid and explained what happened, then finished, "It's to be the Hollow. The boy told me that was where Lobo Colorado's medicine's to be made. He gets the town and the whole of Arizona Territory's going up in flames."

Dusty showed no surprise at the way his friend acted. Full well Dusty knew the strain of Comanche blood which the Kid held down most times. It came to the fore at such times, and it was the blood of Chief Long Walker which made the Kid honor a dead enemy's wish. There were more important matters at stake right now, things which needed attention.

"It'll surely be the Hollow then?" he asked gently.

"Surely so. What're you fixing into do?"

Dusty did not reply immediately. It was a hard decision to make, one few men would have cared for. The town was to be attacked at dawn, and Dusty must decide if he should go back to help, or make for the fort and get the cavalry out. His eyes went to the wagon, to the girls beside it and he shook his head. There was only one way he could play it.

"We couldn't make it back there in time to warn them. Couldn't make it before dawn, not to let the horses rest enough to be of use. Even then we'd likely have to fight our way in. We'd best let the horses rest up for a spell, then push on for Fort Owen as fast as we can go. If we knew the country I'd let you and Waco go on ahead, make better time than we could."

"Sure, but we don't know the lay of the land. You'll likely need all hands and the cook, happen you run into a bunch coming to the fight,'" drawled the Kid. One of the many things the Kid liked about Dusty Fog was the way he made important decisions on the spot. A lesser man might hesitate, call on the others to help make the decision, so that if it went wrong there would be others to blame. That was never the way of Dusty Fog. The decision was his, and his alone, to make. He would make it alone and stand by the consequences, right or wrong.

"I warned them folks back at the Hollow," went on the Kid. "Told them they were likely Lobo Colorado's number one choice when he made war. Told the marshal to fort up that church. Happen he's done it they should be able to hold out until the cavalry can relieve them. If he don't take my word—wal, there's nothing we can do for them, or anybody else, 'cepting for going and burying what's left. It wouldn't do us no good taking the show folks back with us and maybe getting them all killed on the way in."

"Trouble, Captain?" Phyllis asked and joined the two men, carrying two steaming cups of coffee.

"Some," answered Dusty. "I'll get you all together and tell you what the Kid just told me. I want all of you to know what we're up against."

"It's about that town back there, isn't it?" Phyllis asked. "Could we help them if we go back."

"Not as good or as much as a couple of troops of cavalry," Dusty replied, comparing Phyllis with the women of Baptist's Hollow. They'd driven her and her daughters out to risk death at Apache hands. They'd insulted her and her girls, tried to get them jailed. Yet Phyllis was still willing to go back and try to help them out.

He gathered the others and passed on the Kid's words. All eyes were on him as he spoke, and none of the others interrupted. He finished up his review of the situation and told them what they were going to do. Phyllis asked a question:

"What would you do if we weren't with you?"

"Same as we're doing right now, likely. Four men couldn't fight their way in through the Apaches," Dusty replied, then went on. "What arms do you have?"

"Doc's revolver. A ten-gauge. The two rifles Molly uses in her act. Each of the girls has a Derringer."

"Which same's near as many arms as the Confederate Army had in the war," remarked Dusty with a grin. "Can they hit anything with the guns?"

"Hit a running Apache at four feet," Phyllis replied. "Especially if he's running at them."

"*Bueno*. We'll lay up here a piece and let the horses blow, then we'll push on for the fort. Soon as we're clear of the Apaches we'll let the Kid go on ahead."

The rest were satisfied with that. They broke up, and

Molly served out food to them. Thornett sat back with his shoulders resting against the wheel of the wagon, as he so often had in his wandering years. He watched Dusty and nodded in approval. There was a real big man.

Mark's eyes went to Elwin. The young man hardly touched his food, picked at it and stared into the fire. Mark grinned, he could recognize the signs.

"What're you fixing in to do at the fort, friend?" Mark asked. "Join the cavalry?"

Elwin looked up. He'd just been thinking of the same thing himself. It was absurdly easy to pull up stakes and run from his old way of life, but it was not so easy to decide how to live now he'd left. He was painfully aware of his limitations, for working in a town like Baptist's Hollow did not broaden a young man's mind or outlook. There was little Elwin knew about other than serving in a store, and his belly was full of that sort of work. The Army was a choice, although he did not fancy such a life.

"Can't he stay on with us, Doc?" Janice asked, before Elwin could make a reply. "He's a real good juggler."

"Juggler?" said Thornett, eyebrows raising as he looked at Elwin. "We could use a juggler to give a more balanced arrangement to our show. The public gets tired of looking at pretty girls."

"I surely don't," put in Waco, but the others ignored him.

Janice jumped to her feet and went to the wagon, returning with the six cans in her hands. Her face was flushed and eager as she said, "Come on, Elwin, show Doc what you can do."

Elwin gulped, feeling suddenly scared and nervous.

He'd never showed his juggling skill in public, having always been forced to practice in secret. Now he was asked to juggle before a critical audience, with a job hanging in the balance. Then he saw Janice smiling at him, and he felt more confidence. The girl would not want him to show his talent if she did not have faith in him. Taking the cans he got to his feet feeling all eyes on him. For a moment he hesitated, then began to flip the cans into the air. Instantly he forgot the crowd, his full attention being on the flying cans.

Once he'd got his act started Elwin found time to look at the faces of his audience and try to read something from them. In his lack of experience he failed to make anything of how the others looked and sought for a way to take attention from what he imagined were fumbling attempts. There'd been a comedian in the show he saw, and Elwin recalled the jokes told by the man. That might be a way of taking attention from his act. He lost a can by an apparent accident, then recovered it by another equally accidental appearing move.

"I went into Tucson, to a hotel for a meal. The waiter came to my table," Elwin held his voice to a lazy drawl and kept his face dead-pan. "I said, 'Do you have pig's feet?' and he said, 'No, my shoes pinch.' "

The cowhands laughed, so did the girls. They'd all heard that tired joke before, but the way Elwin told it made them laugh. Thornett was not laughing, his face was thoughtful as he watched the cans flying into the air and listened to Elwin tell tired joke after old joke. The laughter of the cowhands did not interest him, they were part of his usual kind of audience and easily amused. It was the laughter of the girls which caught and held Thornett. They were used to seeing skilled comedians and blase about them, yet they were laughing at the tired jokes. Thornett knew why, it was Elwin's unconscious timing which brought the full humor to the act. If the young man could appeal to Phyllis and her girls he would most certainly appeal to less sophisticated tastes.

Elwin juggled on, sending the cans leaping and flying. For the first time in his life he heard the heady sounds of applause. Always in front of him, smiling and looking at him with love in her eyes, was the pretty girl. She inspired him to do his best. He finished the trick by catching the cans on top of each other, all six on his left hand in a pile.

"That was good, friend," said Mark eagerly. "I've never seen it done better."

Thornett nodded in grave agreement. The boy was rough and raw, but he was the finest natural juggler the old showman had ever seen. With a bit of polishing, the right sort of act behind him, Elwin would be a great asset to the show.

"I can do more tricks," Elwin said, worriedly watching the old man.

"Most satisfactory, I'm sure," Thornett answered. "In a career which has brought me into contact with most branches of *the* profession, I have never seen a juggler use such unusual props. I think that if you would embrace the nomadic existence of a traveling showman, there is a great future ahead for you."

"Happen that dust's what I reckon it is," Waco put in, "same future's going to be a mite uncertain."

The rest looked in the direction of his pointing finger, seeing the dust cloud rising from where a side trail ran off into the hills. There was no hesitation in the way Dusty acted. He knew what might be causing that dust and did not intend to be caught unprepared by it.

"Under the wagon, you girls!" he snapped. "Fan out, the rest of you?"

The girls dived under the wagon, flattening down on to the ground, and each taking out her Derringer. Phyllis stopped on her feet long enough to make sure her girls were all armed, then before she took cover herself she saw Elwin was not armed. Calling his name, Phyllis grabbed one of Molly's rifles and tossed it to him, then went under the wagon with her daughters. Elwin levered a bullet into the breech and darted to where Thornett was lying behind the burned-out timbers of an outhouse, the old ten-gauge shotgun in his hands.

The Texans fanned out and took up fighting position fast. They were long used to doing such a thing, and their positions were chosen even as they moved. The result was that while Waco vaulted the sagging corral rails and flattened down, Mark was taking shelter in the charred remains of the station, the Kid flattened down behind a rock and Dusty stayed in a central position. Without needing to be told, the four men got into the best positions to cover each other and protect the wagon.

The Kid lay nestling his rifle and watching the dust. Then he came to his feet to take a closer look at the dust cloud. He relaxed slightly, rifle held across his body and a grin on his face.

Dusty came to his feet, signaling the others to stay where they were. Joining the Kid he also looked at the dust, then asked: "What do you make of it?"

"That's not Apache raisings. Too much dust for that. 'Sides which, Apaches wouldn't stick on a trail," the Kid replied, pausing, then grinning. "Fair bunch of soldiers and a wagon, I reckon."

Dusty relaxed slightly himself now. He knew the Kid's almost amazing eyesight was capable of picking up things beyond anything any of the others could. He did not doubt but that the Kid's guess would prove correct.

"Can you see any more?"

"Caught me a glint of something shiny. No Apache's going to make a fool mistake like that. No more than a big bunch like that'd stick to a trail. They'd be off it, in the bushes there, so the dust wouldn't show. And there's a wagon with them. I figger it's either a detail headed for the fort, or coming out from it," the Kid replied. "Was I asked, that is."

"Take it you're asked," grunted Dusty. "What else can you see?"

Dusty could make out the faint shapes by now, but he wouldn't have wanted to bet his life on their being white or Apache. He saw the Kid grinning and knew his keen-eyed young friend saw something more. It was some moments before the Kid spoke, then he indicated the shape at the head of the rest.

"Mind that man riding out front?"

Dusty squinted his eyes and tried to make out who the man in front was. He'd always admired the Kid's long vision, and this was another example of it. Five minutes dragged by before Dusty could make out who the point rider of the advancing party was. When he did, Dusty felt relieved.

The man at the front of the approaching party was a big, burly figure in the uniform of a United States cavalryman, a sergeant. His brick-red face could only belong to an Irishman, and his campaign hat was shoved back from short-cropped red hair. It was a face Dusty knew well, and the sergeant rode in a manner

Dusty knew all too well. He slouched in his saddle, Springfield carbine across his knees, eyes flickering in each direction.

Seeing the way Sergeant Paddy Magoon rode, Dusty knew there was bad trouble in the air. Magoon learned Indian fighting against the Sioux and Cheyenne to the north, the Comanche and Kiowa to the east; and was now taking a post-graduate course against the wildest, most savage of them all, the Apaches. Magoon knew Indians, could read the signs and Magoon was full ready for war.

The approaching party consisted of Magoon and some twenty men, counting the rear-guard of a corporal and four men. They surrounded a wagon, a big Army wagon, driven by a large shape in a sleeveless, dark blue shirt, cavalry trousers and boots, and with a Stetson hat drawn down to shield the face.

A mischievous grin came to Dusty's face. "Magoon!" he roared out. "You drunken Irish wastrel! Sit erect in that saddle, you look like a loose-tied sack of cowdung."

The troopers riding under Magoon's command expected to see their sergeant explode into sudden and violent action, for he was no man to allow a stranger, and a civilian to boot, to make fun of him. Instead of leaping from his saddle and hurling the impertinent, small cowhand clear over the burned-out relay station, Magoon sat stiff and straight. His posture could not have been more correct and according to the drill manual had he been passing Generals Grant, Sheridan and Crook all in one group. His rugged Irish face twisted in a grin of pure delight, and turning he bellowed at his troopers:

"Darlin's! 'Tis me ould friend, Captain Fog, who've you've heard me talk about so often. Now sit yourselves up straight and try to look like cavalrymen, or by gob, he'll be making you. Sit up now, and don't be disgracing your poor ould sergeant in front of Cap'n Fog."

Dusty held his carbine in his left hand and stepped forward to greet Magoon. The big sergeant's dismount came straight out of the drill manual. He snapped into a smart brace and brought off a salute which would have done credit to the drill instructor at West Point. Then he took Dusty's hand in his, the smile on his face and the warmth of his grip showing his delight at meeting his hero once more. For Dusty Fog was very much a hero to this hard-drinking, hard-fighting sergeant of cavalry. He'd been Magoon's hero ever since he took over a leaderless, demoralized battalion of cavalry and turned them into an efficient, proud, fighting unit. The fact that in doing so Dusty also saved Magoon from a court-martial did nothing to detract from his merits in the big sergeant's eyes.

"You're a long ways from home, Paddy," greeted Dusty, his hand tingling from the other's grip.

"Been over to Fort Beckett, Cap'n. Lootenant took sick with the fever and left me in charge."

Dusty did not think much about the words, not at the moment. Fort Beckett was the main base for the army in Arizona. It was General Crook's headquarters and the supply point for the other forts. There was nothing unusual in a wagon being sent to Fort Beckett, except the size of the escort. A lieutenant, a sergeant and twenty men seemed a little superfluous unless trouble was expected, or the load was important.

"Seen any Apaches?" Dusty inquired, glancing at the

big wagon, at the knots of the canvas cover. They were waxed over and bore an official seal.

"More than a bit, Cap'n," replied Magoon seriously. "They're up and painted for war, or I've never seen a bad Indian. We ran into the track of a big bunch and cut over this way to try and get the folks out. Looks like we got here too late to help."

"The Kid allows they got clear there a week back. What's in the wagon?"

"Damned if I know, Cap'n. 'Twas all very secret and mysterious. We was sent off in a helluva rush. The lootenant might have known but he never said a word if he did. Anyways, he took down with fever and may the devil sleep on his pillow every night. He was the damned fool who shot down ole Ramon. We left for Beckett eight days back. Right after the court-martial."

Ideas were running through Dusty's head. Ideas half formed and discarded for lack of men to make them work. The Apaches were up, and it looked as if every tribe were sending men to see if the medicine of this new leader was good. If they could be held and the attack of Baptist's Hollow was to fail, there would be no uprising. The braves would fade back to their own people, and even Lobo Colorado's own tribe would not follow a leader after his medicine went bad.

With these twenty men at his back, Dusty knew he could fight his way into Baptist's Hollow. He would come in behind the Apaches after they started their dawn attack, charge in on them and either break the attack or get through to hold the church. With twenty men like these, backed by his three friends, Dusty knew he could hold the church until reinforcements from Fort Owen arrived.

It was something to think about. Dusty was not in the

Army, in fact, never had served officially with the Union Army. He'd no right to take these men from their duty or make any plans in which they formed a part. For all that, he meant to try out his idea. Magoon would follow him, he knew that, would risk court-martial if Dusty said the word. If they succeeded it would break up the great uprising before it properly got under way. If they failed—Well, it wasn't likely they'd be around for the Army to take action against. Lobo Colorado would see to that. He and his warhunting warriors.

The other members of Dusty's party were emerging now that they saw there was no danger. Magoon beamed in delight and advanced to scoop Phyllis up into his big arms and kiss her hard.

"Phyllis, me ould darling," he whooped. "Sure and you look more beautiful every time I see you. When're you going to marry me, so's we can raise the finest fighting family in the world?"

"I'll think about it," Phyllis replied, shoving Magoon away from her. "If you muss up my hair I'll flatten you. Who've you got to match against me this time, Paddy, Calamity Jane?"

"A gal who'd make Calam look like a powder puff," answered Magoon, then turned to where the driver of the wagon was swinging down. "Hey, Big Em, come over here and shake hands with Madam Fiona."

The driver turned and removed the Stetson. Phyllis bit down a gulp as she saw long black hair fall to a pair of wide shoulders. She'd thought the driver was a man and a big one at that. Now she found herself looking into a pair of laughing, Irish blue eyes and a large, but pretty Irish face. Big Em, pride of Fort Owen, stepped forward, holding out her right hand to Phyllis. She was big all around. Her hard muscled figure strained at the shirt and pants she wore, her arms bulged with powerful muscles.

"Howdy, Madam," she greeted, her brogue almost thick enough to be cut with a knife. "Sure, and I thought you'd be bigger than you are. I was looking forward to licking you."

"I've licked bigger than you," Phyllis sniffed, taking one hand.

"Have ye now?" purred Big Em. A glint of battle came into her eyes. She loved fighting as much as did Phyllis. "Well, we can soon see about that——"

"I think we had best wait until the Apaches are settled first, ladies," Thornett put in mildly, for he knew Phyllis was capable of pitching right into Big Em.

"Doc's called it right," smiled Phyllis. "We'll have to wait. Anyway, we don't want to spoil the fun for the boys at Fort Owen, do we?"

"Devil a bit of it," agreed Big Em, grinning back at Phyllis. "I can wait. But there'll be none of your holding pennies game for me. Toe to toe we stand until you're whipped."

"I wouldn't have it any other way," Phyllis answered. "Coffee's on the boil, come and have a cup."

"I'd drink coffee any time. Did you ever meet Calamity Jane, Madam?"

The two women strolled away, discussing fighting in the way townswomen might exchange gossip or recipes. Phyllis knew one thing, she was going to have the fight of her life on her hands when she met Big Em.

Dusty gathered the soldiers and his three friends around him, then began to tell them of his plan. The cavalrymen all sat silent and listened, for they'd heard Magoon talk of this small, insignificant-looking Texan as if he were a god. Dusty hid nothing from them and warned of the dangers they would run. If they failed, court-martial was certain, death more than likely. If they succeeded there was a chance of preventing an uprising which would cost thousands of lives and millions of dollars.

"What're you aiming to do then, Cap'n, darlin'?" asked Magoon, although knowing Dusty, he could guess.

"Take your men to the town. Either break the attack, or hold the church until relief can be brought from Fort Owen," Dusty replied.

"My idea is that we come on them just after they hit the town. Go in like the devil after a yearling, screaming fit to bust and shooting straight. Smash through with the wagons, men ready to cut out any team hoss that goes down. With luck we would smash through before they get over their surprise."

CHAPTER SEVEN

Reinforcements from the Stockade

So it was decided without fuss or bother. A bold, desperate stroke to end a bloody Apache uprising and save a territory.

Dusty's plan was simple, very simple. It would work, given luck and the folk at Baptist's Hollow doing the right thing. The party would pull out after dark, the Ysabel Kid having scouted to make sure no Apache was watching them. Then they would travel through the night towards the town, the horses would be rested then and make good time. At dawn, when Lobo Colorado and his men were attacking Baptist's Hollow, Dusty's bunch would fall on them from the rear.

In the unlikely event that only a relatively small bunch of Apaches were involved, the surprise attack would scatter and break them. There was little chance of being so few that Dusty could drive them off. Lobo Colorado would see to that. His men were bunched in number, enough to make sure they could take the town. So Dusty hoped his attack would smash through and allow them to make the church.

Looking at the men who would accompany him on this desperate venture, Dusty felt satisfied he'd got the best possible for his plan. Mark, the Kid and Waco were fighting men from soda to hock. They'd fought along-side him often enough for Dusty to know he could rely on them to follow his lead into anything. Magoon's men looked competent enough. Most of them looked like veterans who'd fought Apaches and knew how to handle themselves. Only two gave the appearance of being recruits, but even those two showed no signs of panic at the thought of action. Big Em was a freighter, a good one. She'd been seated on a wagon box almost from the time she could walk and was capable of han-dling her team in the face of an Apache attack. She'd done so more than once that Dusty knew of, for he re-membered hearing of her from soldiers who knew her well. Thornett's show gave Dusty no worries. The old doctor was as brave as a lion, cool and battle-sure. Phyllis was brave and would not lose her head, while the girls were just as steady, even Rosie.

For all of that it was a small enough force for a man to try and halt a full-scale Apache uprising. That was just what they were trying to do. They were throwing themselves into the brunt of the Apache attack, trying to stem the tide before it could rise to full and flood the Arizona territory in death and destruction. It was for this purpose Dusty was taking so desperate a chance. In the spirit of the men who stayed at, and fought, the Alamo, Dusty was preparing to risk a few to save many.

"It'll go hard for you if we miss out, Paddy," Dusty remarked as they stood side by side and watched the camp settling down to rest.

"Sure, Cap'n," agreed Magoon, although he could not see any plan Dusty made going wrong. "But we won't be around to see it."

Dusty's eyes went to the big wagon again. "I'd like to

see what you're toting that needs so many men for escort.''

''Would you now?'' Magoon answered, dipping his hand into his pocket and taking out a clasp knife. He opened the blade and stepped forward. ''I'll soon tell you, Cap'n, darlin'.''

''Sergeant!'' Dusty barked out, the note in his voice bringing Magoon to a dead stop. ''What were your orders about that load?''

''Deliver it to the fort unopened.''

''Then just what do you think you're going to do?''

Magoon looked sheepish. ''Only aimed to pry the corners up a mite, Cap'n.''

Dusty relaxed and grinned. It was rare that Magoon ever showed respect for any officer. Yet he treated Dusty with complete respect, even though the only uniform the small Texan ever wore belonged to an enemy army. Dusty was about to make some remark, but there was an interruption.

Magoon's bosom friend, erstwhile fellow sergeant, now reduced to corporal, Tolitski, had set their men out as pickets. One of these pickets was now on his feet and pointing along the stage trail. His voice sounded excited, for he was one of the recruits.

''Soldiers coming!'' he yelled. ''Party from the fort, looks like.''

Dusty and Magoon were the first to reach the trooper. They looked at the approaching party. Dusty was disappointed at seeing so small a party, although he hoped it would have an officer along. If that was the case Dusty could lay the whole thing in the officer's lap and leave Magoon clear of responsibility. Magoon recognized the riders and gave an annoyed, angry growl.

"That's just about all we need," he said, looking at the big, hulking three-bar who rode at the head of the party. "That's Bogran from the stockade. Looks like he's been collecting prisoners from the forts."

The party came closer and Dusty looked the big man over. Sergeant Borgran was heavy-set, big and with a hard, cruel face. It was not the face of a martinet disciplinarian. It was the face of a savage brute who took a delight in punishing. He rode in a slouching way that made Dusty's hackles rise. The seat was sloppy and hard on the horse. He was not a light rider and probably a cruel one.

Behind the sergeant came four men, bare-headed, hand-cuffed, and riding in pairs. The rear was brought up by two big, hulking, brutish-looking corporals. They were hard-looking men, faces showing the same love of cruelty as did the sergeant's. Each of the three non-coms, wore a long-barrelled Peacemaker in an open-topped holster, a stout club hung at the right side of their belts and a Springfield butt showed from under their legs. They were well armed and for a purpose, they were taking the other four to the Stockade, the military prison. All in all the three men were typical of the kind chosen to act as warders at the Stockade. Men selected for their brute strength and savage ways. A Stockade non-com was not a job which called for kindness, and they'd little regard for human life or suffering. Bogran was spoken of throughout the Army as being the worst of a bad bunch. Some of the guards occasionally showed a spark of humanity and decency, but he never did. Bogran was hated from Montana to the Mexican border and reveled in that hatred. It was such a reputation that was invaluable to him. It carried him from trooper to senior Stockade sergeant and, he hoped, would carry him to a commission and command of a Stockade.

Bringing his horse to a halt with a cruel jerk at its mouth, Bogran looked at Magoon with dislike in his eyes. Bogran hated Magoon, and every other serving soldier, regarded them as possible candidates for the Stockade. He knew the Irish sergeant did not like him and reveled in the thought.

"What's all this, Magoon?" he asked.

"What're you doing out of your cage, Bogran?" growled Magoon in reply. "I thought they only let you out when there wasn't a chance of you polluting the air decent soldiers breathe."

Bogran never worried about insults, they rolled off a hide which was thicker than a California redwood tree. He jerked a contemptuous finger towards his prisoners. "I was sent to collect this bunch. What's doing here?"

"Sergeant," Dusty Fog said, moving forward. "Why are those men handcuffed?"

The sneer left Bogran's face. He knew that tone of voice. It was the tone of a real tough officer. The sort of officer who would allow no disrespect. Then the sneer came back again as he looked Dusty over. Here was no officer. Just a small cowhand, a nobody.

"They're prisoners, sonny——"

"Sonny, is it?" bellowed Magoon, outraged that anyone should speak in such a manner to his hero. "This here's Cap'n Fog. So watch your damned, stupid lip or he'll be making you wish you had."

The sneer wavered for a moment. Bogran knew Magoon of old, knew how little respect he had for any man's rank. For Magoon to take such an attitude meant that here was a man he respected. This small man wearing cowhand's clothes meant something to Magoon. The fact that he was wearing civilian clothes meant nothing. Many an officer traveled out of uniform. Some of them even affected cowhand dress, although few wore it with the ease and assurance of the small Texan. Bogran studied Dusty. There was a military bearing about him, the undefinable something which marked down a real tough, efficient officer to the eyes of a soldier.

Dusty's voice was low, but there was something in it which wiped the sneer from Bogran's face. "Sergeant, even *you* should know a prisoner is released in time of action. And sergeant, the way things are standing with the Apaches, action is coming up."

Ignoring the crowd who were gathering at his back, Dusty looked along the line of prisoners. Three of them were what he expected, drunks, malcontents and trouble-causers all of them. The other prisoner was not of that kind. He was a slim, dark, good-looking young man. His uniform was well-cut and on the sleeves marks where chevrons had been. Dusty recognized this man, so did Mark Counter. He was Chet Bronson, an ex-captain of Bushrod Sheldon's Confederate Cavalry, and had been Mark's commanding officer in the war.

Bronson was what was known as a turn-back, a man who gave up his officer status to stay in the Union Army, come West and fight Indians. He was a good soldier, a fine shot, a peerless horseman and known as a first-rate scout. He should never be here, with these hard-bargains, candidates for the hell-hole which was the Army Stockade.

"That's right, is it?" Bogran growled, regaining some of his composure. He turned and bellowed an order for the prisoners to dismount, swung down from his horse and walked towards them. "I'd be better off with the Apaches than with this scum loose. Wouldn't I, Bronson?"

Chet Bronson stood rigid and did not reply as the hulking man stopped in front of him. More than any other kind of prisoner Bogran hated a non-com who was put into the Stockade and went out of his way to abuse such as came to him. Bogran was not a man to be thwarted by silence and knew how to handle it. The back of his hand lashed across Bronson's face, staggering him into the horses.

"Answer me, you lousy, reb turnback——!" Bogran began.

A hand gripped Bogran's collar, hauling him backwards. The crowd would have never thought so small a man as Dusty Fog packed such strength, for the huge sergeant was thrown backwards and almost fell. He caught his balance and let out an almost animal roar of rage. For all his anger Bogran was cautious. He was no gunman and knew that the small Texan was his master in any matter which involved the exchange of Colt courtesies. With that in mind Bogran's hand fanned down towards his club and he hurled himself bodily at the small man.

Dusty moved faster than the eye could follow, almost. He dived forward, under Bogran's club, caught the man's right leg and hauled it from the ground. Bogran's other foot was in the air, striding forward when his right lost the earth. He let out an angry yell, lost his club and went down, flailing the air with his arms and smashed down hard.

To one side of Dusty the two Stockade corporals prepared to help their sergeant. The first to move learned his lesson fast for Mark Counter caught his arm, turned him and shot out a fist. It was a beautiful blow, the mighty army muscles throwing the fist, arm shooting out with the full weight of Mark's body behind it. The punch connected squarely with the side of the corporal's jaw, his head snapped to one side and he seemed to take wings. It was the sort of blow which ended a fight before things got going. The corporal smashed down, bounced once and lay without a move.

The second corporal let out a bellow, saw Bogran was getting up and turned to avenge his friend. Mark heard Waco's yell of warning and thrust the impetuous youngster to one side. Then Mark attacked. It was a sight to gladden the heart of any soldier, the way Mark took that Stockade corporal. The man's hand was fanning down for his club, but even as it slid clear Mark slammed a punch into his middle. Gasping in pain the corporal let the club fall and swung a wild, round-house blow at Mark. There was plenty of steam, weight and muscle behind the blow, but there was only one trouble. It never landed.

Mark fought in a way which was a joy to behold. He kept his fist up, left held protectively across his body, right moving as it looked for an opening. All the time Mark moved in fast, bouncing steps, keeping his feet the same distance apart. The corporal was as big as Mark, slightly heavier and at least as strong, but he was a plain swinger with neither skill nor science. In other such encounters the Stockade guard relied on brute strength and that was of no use against a man like Mark Counter. The wild swinging blows either missed, or were brushed aside by Mark's guard, then his other hand shot out with savage power. The corporal was tough and hard, but mere toughness was no use. His mouth and nose were running blood and his eye swelling, but he'd never laid a hand on Mark.

There was no mercy in the way Mark took that Stockade non-com, for such men never showed mercy to any prisoner under them. Then Mark got his opening. Like a Missouri mule-kick his left sank almost wrist deep into the corporal's middle. The man let out a croaking grunt of agony and sank to his knees. His hand went to the butt of his gun, lifting it clear of leather.

That was when Mark Counter got riled. The fight had been fair so far and Mark refrained from using any of the rough-house tricks he'd learned in a dozen such brawls. When he saw the man drawing the revolver, he lost his temper. Jumping forward Mark drove up his foot in a savage, dynamite packed kick which exploded under the man's jaw. The big corporal was almost lifted to his feet, and from the way his neck snapped back Mark thought he'd killed him. The corporal went right over, crashing down and lying without a move. Mark turned to see if there was anything he could do to help Dusty and found his help was not needed.

Coming up to his feet, Bogran lunged forward with arms ready to clamp hold of, and crush the life from, Dusty. Dusty did not even move to avoid the grip, but before the arms could enfold him he acted. Using the deadly karate technique which made up for his lack of inches, Dusty brought up his foot and drove it out. The high heel of the riding boot smashed just under Bogran's kneecap, driving home with brutal force and doubling the man over as he clutched at the injured part. The kick was enough to cripple him, but the extra pain caused by the high heel of the boot did all Dusty hoped it would.

Bogran was doubled over, holding his knee, face twisted in agony. He was all but helpless for Dusty's

next attack, which came with the speed which made
Dusty famous. Dusty's right hand lashed around,
fingers straight and rigid, thumb bent over his palm, in
the *tegatana*, the handsword. The base of the palm
caught Bogran with smashing force at the side of his
neck, just behind the ear. He went down like a back-
broke rabbit, landing on his face, hands clawing into the
ground. His pain-twisted face looked up at the small
Texan, then his fingers touched something hard and
cold. It was the butt of the Stockade corporal's revolver, lying where it fell after Mark rendered its owner
incapable of using it, or anything else, for some time.
Bogran's hand closed on the revolver butt, and Dusty
jumped forward. Driving his left hand into Bogran's
long, lank black hair, Dusty heaved the man upwards
with a pull which almost scalped him and lifted him
clear to his knees. Bogran's howl of agony died off as
Dusty swung his other hand, using the *Uraken*, the
back-fist. The hand came round, powered by Dusty's
steel hard muscles, the protruding base joint of the second finger crashing into the man's temple. Bogran's
howl died off, and his huge body went limp.

There was excited chatter among the watchers. Waco
was abusing Mark in no uncertain manner for making
him miss a good fight while the Kid stood grinning. The
soldiers and Big Em were clearly delighted, although at
any other time they would have been all for the Army
men in a fight with civilians. The Stockade guards were
in a different class and did not count as Army in the eyes
of the soldiers. Only one person was not in that excited,
wildly gesticulating, talking group.

Phyllis stood back from the others, her face sober and
thoughtful. She knew there must be some trickery and
secret skill in the way Dusty handled Bogran, but there

was nothing of that nature in how Mark took the corporal. Phyllis knew more than a little about fist-fight-
ing, male as well as female. She knew that the average
pugilist was simply a wild swinger who won only if he
could hit harder and take more punishment than his op-
ponent. It was the same with the girl fighters she'd met.
They copied the men. Yet she'd heard rumors of a new
fighting style which was supplanting the old toe-to-toe
method. This way of Mark's must be the new style, and
with it he could take any pugilist she'd ever seen.

Her eyes went to Big Em, noting the size of the
woman and the big, muscle-packed arms. Phyllis was no
fool. She knew the fighting game well. Big Em, under
the old style of fighting, had everything in her favor;
youth, strength, size and reach. Phyllis knew that her
own extra knowledge and experience could hardly off-
set all the disadvantages. Her only hope was to have a
talk with Mark Counter and learn all she could from
him before the fight.

Dusty turned his attention to business again, looking
at Magoon who was beaming enough to set the grass on
fire. "Release the prisoners, Sergeant."

For once in his life Paddy Magoon hesitated before
obeying an order given to him by Dusty Fog. He knew
one of the prisoners and could guess at the kind the
other two were. He was willing to allow Bronson to go
free, for Magoon did not regard the southerner as a
prisoner, but not the others. He stood for an instant,
without moving to obey, then said:

"Reckon we should, cap'n?" He indicated the big,
sullen-looking man who'd been riding next to Bronson.
"Harris there's in for life, killed a sergeant in a drunken
brawl. I don't know about the other two, but with the
shortage of recruits, they don't get sent to the Stockade

if there's any chance of them making something."

Dusty did not reply to Magoon. He looked the men over then spoke, "I'm releasing you now and when we ride tonight you'll each be given a carbine and twenty bullets. If we're attacked while we're here you'll be armed, if not you'll get the carbine just before we pull out. See to it, Sergeant Magoon. Take the carbines from your three best pistol shots. I'll attend to Bronson myself. The three men will ride with your detail, where the Stockade non-coms can keep an eye on them." He looked back at the men. "You'd best all know this. The Apaches are up, out in force. The whole country's swarming with them, and you won't get a mile if you run. If the Apaches don't get you, my men will. At the end of the trouble you will be handed over to Sergeant Bogran again."

"Big deal," growled Harris sullenly, his eyes dropping to the revolver on the ground.

"It's the only deal you rate in your present position, soldier," snapped Dusty. "And a better one than you'd get with Bogran. But if you want it that way I'll let him and his men take you on to the Stockade right now."

"We'll ride with you," grunted Harris. He was under no doubt as to what his chances would be with Bogran. If they ran into Apache trouble and things became in any way dangerous, Bogran would not hesitate. He would leave the prisoners as bait to slow down the Apaches and make good his escape. This way, by staying with Dusty Fog's party, there was a chance of escaping either on the trail in the darkness, or after the fighting was over.

"Then you ride under my terms," replied Dusty and turned to Magoon. "Release these men, Sergeant. Keep them under escort all the time, except for Chet Bronson.

I want to talk with him. And Sergeant," Dusty saw the gleam in Harris's eyes. "See you collect the Stockade noncoms' weapons. They might give somebody ideas."

For a moment Harris's face darkened in anger, then a smile came to it. He did not know who this small, soft-talking Texan was; knew nothing except that he acted and talked like a tough officer who knew what he was doing; but he was no man's fool. Harris stood while his handcuffs were removed. He watched Corporal Tolitski collecting Bogran and the unconscious corporal's side-arms and shrugged. That revolver which Tolitski picked up had formed part of Harris's escape plan. Now it was out of his reach.

Bronson walked with Dusty to where the Texans' saddles lay. Dusty bent and drew his carbine from the boot, passing it to the dark man. Then opening his saddle pouch, Dusty removed a box of bullets for the gun and gave them to Bronson.

"Sorry I don't have a spare handgun along, Chet," said Dusty. "The carbine's the best I can do for you. It's full loaded. How come you're in with this bunch?"

"I'm going to the Stockade—for thirty years."

Dusty looked hard at the soldier. Mark was by his side now and stared at Bronson, hardly able to believe his ears. Bronson was a soldier and a good one, the two knew his reputation both in the war and since. He was a natural, a born leader of men and could have risen to officer status, but he would not accept the bars in the Union Army. It did not seem possible he could commit so serious a military offence as to warrant that punishment.

"How'd it come about?" Mark asked, for he was an old friend, a comrade in arms. He could ask a personal question such as this without offending Bronson.

"Called it striking an officer in the face of the enemy."

"He must have pushed you hard before you'd do that," Dusty observed.

"Could say that, although the court-martial didn't," replied Bronson. There was just a touch of bitterness in his voice. "I was riding scout for the troop that hit Ramon's camp. There was a shave-tail lieutenant in command, fresh out from the Point and a real Indian-hater. Our patrol was headed across the reservation. There were rumors that Lobo Colorado and his bunch had held meetings with other tribes, and the colonel wanted to know about it. The lieutenant sent me out on a point and took the patrol on. I heard shooting and headed for it, right into Ramon's village. I tell you, that boy went kill crazy. He was off his hoss and lining his gun on an old squaw's head, just going to shoot her. I hit him to stop him and got the troop out. Back at the fort he had me arrested, tossed in the guard-house and charged me with striking him. He made out I took him wrong and laid the blame for the whole thing on me. The troop were all recruits. They didn't know sic 'em about what was happening, so the court-martial was forced to take things at their face value. I reckon they didn't believe his story, but they had to stand by the brass. I'd have been shot otherwise." He looked down at the carbine in his hands. "Thirty years in the Stockade. I'd rather been shot."

Dusty nodded towards the other three prisoners. "How about them?"

"Taller and Morgan are snow-birds who got caught," Bronson replied. A snow-bird was a man who enlisted in the Army when winter was coming on and deserted in the spring. "Harris, well he's the sort you get. A real good fighting man and a good soldier in action, but no good when there is none. He was on a small post and killed his trooper sergeant in a drunken fight. I don't know the full story of it, but I knew the sergeant, and I don't reckon Harris was all to blame. You watch him, Dusty, and Bogran won't get to Baptist's Hollow alive. Bogran's been riding Harris all the time, telling what's going to happen to him at the Stockade, trying to make him run. You'd have done better to leave us tied."

"Us?" Dusty repeated gently.

"Me and Harris at least. Give us half a chance and we'll both be gone."

"No, you won't, Chet," answered Dusty. "You're a soldier, a good one. You've seen Apaches on the rampage before now and know what they can do. You know what this rising means to the folks in Arizona territory, it'll end this part of the world for another twenty years. You'll stick by us."

Molly walked up to them. "How about bringing your friend to the fire, Dusty?" she asked. "We've coffee on the boil, and he looks like he could drink some."

Bronson followed Dusty to the medicine show fire. The carbine hung heavily in his hands, the box of bullets bulging his pocket. His regular mount stood near at hand, a big, powerful horse which won plenty of money in the fort races. Once on the horse he would stand a better than fair chance of escape, even matched with the Ysabel Kid's white stallion.

Then Bronson looked at Molly, at her sisters sitting at the fire, then back at Dusty Fog. He cursed himself for a stupid fool. This was no time to be thinking of others. For all that, he knew he would. He could imagine the girls when the Apaches got through with them. Like Dusty said, he'd seen Apache work on men, women and children. He could not leave these girls to face such a death. Bronson tried to tell himself this was his sole reason for staying on, but he knew he was lying to himself. He was too much a soldier to desert his duty.

Dusty introduced Bronson to the girls, noticing the way the soldier held Molly's hand just a shade longer than was necessary. At other times he would have regarded this as a normal thing, a man showing a keen eye for a pretty girl. Under the prevailing circumstances it was no use. The girls accepted Bronson. They'd seen him come into the camp with the other prisoners, but that meant nothing to them. If he was all right with Dusty Fog, the girls were willing to accept him.

Across the open space Bogran was sitting up, moaning and holding his head. He forced himself on to his feet and staggered to Big Em's wagon and pulled the dipper from the water-keg on the side. He soaked his head in the water, then swung around, hand clawing at his empty holster.

"I've got it, Bogran!"

Bogran turned to meet Paddy Magoon's mocking eyes. He took the revolver held out to him, and his hate-filled eyes turned to where Dusty Fog was standing talking to Bronson. His hand shook as he held the revolver, for Bogran was in a rage almost beyond controlling. "I'll kill that shortgrowed bitch," he snarled.

"You just now tried," scoffed Magoon. "He bested you with his bare hands and no trouble to it. You go against him with a gun and he'll not even bother to kill you. He'll just smash both the knees of you, he's that fast."

"Who is he, Magoon?" snarled Bogran. "Is he Army?"

"Do you think I'd touch me hat to any man who

wasn't the best damned fighting officer alive?'' Magoon demanded. He never regarded Dusty as a civilian. "You talk soft, easy and real polite around him, Bogran. He's a kind and gentle man unless he's roused—and you haven't seen him roused yet.''

Bogran watched Magoon walk away and started to say something, then shut his mouth. Magoon was no man to give respect because of rank, only where such respect was well merited. This small man must be someone of importance. It was something for Bogran to think about. There was a fast growing group of officers who were trying to stamp out the brutalities of the Stockades. This might be one of that group, and Bogran knew his actions were wide open to question. If the small man was of the group trying to end Bogran's way of running the Stockade, he'd seen too much right here. Bogran slouched to his conscious corporal and squatted down with him, snarling a curse to the man's inquiry after his health. Bogran had reached a decision. Somehow, some time, real soon, that small man must die.

Soon after, while the girls prepared a meal, Dusty called his three friends, Magoon, Thornett, Big Em and Bogran to him. Bogran came sullenly and squatted down to listen to what was said. For all his hatred of Dusty, the Stockade sergeant had to admit there was little in detail he missed. Duties were allocated so that everyone of them knew what to do and what the others would be doing. There was only one interruption. It came when Dusty was telling of the Kid, Waco and Bronson as scouts.

"Bronson's a prisoner," growled Bogran.

"And he's the best scout we've got," replied Dusty. "Unless you'd like to take the point, Sergeant.''

Bogran's angry growl could have meant anything, but

he did not offer to take the risky duty of riding on ahead as scout. With the objection dealt with, Dusty went on making his arrangements.

Doc's wagon'll be a mite crowded, so you'll have to take the injured Stockade corporal on your wagon box, Miss Em. Sit him between you and Phyl.''

"Yo!" Big Em gave the cavalry reply, even though she did not wish to have any part of helping a Stockade guard.

"Sergeant Magoon," said Dusty, a thought coming to him. "Pick out a good man. I'm sending a message to the fort to tell them what we're doing. Take the best man you've got, other than Corporal Tolitski. I need him here.''

"I'll send Crayhill, he's rode despatch before now and knows the country," answered Magoon and called a tall man with long tawny hair, side whiskers and huge moustache.

Dusty told the man what he wanted done, then got a pencil and paper from Thornett and settled down to compose a letter to the commanding officer of Fort Owen.

Fifteen minutes later, after a meal, Crayhill was riding out, headed overland for the fort. The rest settled down to wait until it was time to move out, all relaxing except for the alert and watchful pickets.

Phyllis got her chance to have a talk with Mark. The result was partly satisfying to her even though there was no chance of doing more than talk at the moment. She found herself helping hitch the team to Big Em's wagon before she could more than talk with Mark. With that done she went to her daughters and warned them about how they should act on the following day. On her way back she came face to face with Corporal Tolitski, an old friend from other Army camps. They'd not managed to find time to speak with each other before this and she smiled.

"How'd you lose it this time, Ranko?" she asked, indicating the mark where a third stripe had been stitched.

"Celebrating," Tolitski replied with a grin. Losing and gaining his third stripe was no novelty to him. "You mind that big Osage squaw of Ring Goodwin?"

"Sure," agreed Phyllis. "You matched me against her and lost two month's pay betting her to win."

"I did," Tolitski answered. "Well, she took on Big Em toe-to-toe."

"Who won?"

"Big Em. Took her easy in fifteen rounds."

Phyllis gulped down something which suddenly seemed to block her throat. Tolitski was called away at that moment, and Phyllis was more than worried when she went to Big Em's wagon. In her fight with Ring Goodwin's Osage squaw she'd taken twenty hard fought rounds to win and considered herself very lucky to have done so at all. If Em won easily in fifteen rounds Phyllis was in bad trouble.

Now more than ever, Phyllis knew she must learn Mark's system of fighting.

CHAPTER EIGHT

Night at Baptist's Hollow

Major Ellwood was in a vile mood when he returned to the jail with food for his prisoners. It was dark, and he was late in feeding the two men in the cells, but he'd just finished the exhausting task of getting his people to the rifle pits. It was a hard task, and only by being strenuously unpleasant was Ellwood able to get all the first party into position. Man after man had tried to think up an excuse to avoid doing his civic duty, but Ellwood ruled them all out and, by threatening to jail any absentee, drew his men. He knew he would probably have the same trouble with the second watch and did not relish going around in the middle of the night to find them.

One of the chief causes of complaint was that the miners were not forced to take on full responsibility for the defense of the town. It was typical of the mentality of the Baptist's Hollow citizen that he thought those men from the hills should be forced to defend the town.

In all fairness Ellwood tried to get the miners interested in his idea, for all were good shots, cool and brave men. They would have stiffened his line of defense if they would agree to help out. Individually and collectively the miners refused to have any part in those holes in the ground. Ellwood might have read a sinister warning in the refusal, but he was in no mood to look beyond surface appearance. What he did know was that the miners were ready to leave town, chancing the open country, rather than fight in the rifle pits. That was the last thing he wanted. If Lobo Colorado and his men came, the miners would be a fighting force worth having.

Scully and Willy looked at the tray of food Ellwood brought to them. It was a decent meal and struck them both as an ominous sign. They were capable of putting two and two together and making the answer come out correct. The arrival of the miners, their lack of celebrating, taken with odd scraps of conversation from outside the jail, added up to one thing. Apache trouble in its worst form.

"I hear you've got Apache trouble, Major," said Scully, as he took the tray through the slot in the bars. "Me'n Willy can both use a rifle. Be pleased to help."

"I bet you would," Ellwood snapped back. "If I let you out, you'd be gone before morning."

"With Apaches on the warpath, without horses—afoot?" asked Scully, looking mildly reproving. "Marshal, I don't like your stuffy, pious little town and wish to be out of it, never to return, but not at the moment. I'd go further. I'd rather be here than out there right now."

Ellwood snorted. Suddenly he realized he was beginning to think and act like a citizen of Baptist's Hollow, beginning to suspect every motive as being the worst. He felt suddenly sick of the whole business, of this town where religious feeling was corrupted to mean distrust, bias, suspicion and prejudice. The feeling made him angry at himself and unreasoning in his anger, knowing that he was in the wrong.

The two prisoners could have been released earlier and allowed to work on the rifle pits. The charges against them would be covered by a fine, and Scully held enough cash to pay it, so there was no reason for him to hold them. Now, in his cross-grained, unreasoning anger, he would not allow them to leave the cells, even to help guard the town. Turning on his heel Ellwood went towards the door.

"Hey, Marshal!" Willy said, his drawl speeded up until it was almost whizzing along. "You ain't going to leave us locked in here when there's likely to be Apaches jumping us any time."

"I'll let you out if the attack comes, not before," Ellwood snapped, then he went out of the jail, slamming and locking the office door.

Ellwood regretted his actions as soon as he turned the key in the lock but would not give way and admit it. He turned and received something of a shock as two dark, tall shapes loomed up before him. Taken by surprise at the silent approach of the miners, Zeke and Ike, Ellwood dropped his hand towards the butt of his gun and stepped back a pace.

"Easy there, Major, it's us," Zeke growled. "You ain't changed your mind yet, have you?"

"About what?"

"The way you're handling things here," answered Zeke, his waved hand taking in the circle of the town and the rifle pits.

Ellwood read an implication in the words that was not there. He knew the miners did not approve of the way he was defending the town and took the wrong attitude.

Shaking his head he snapped, "I'm handling things the way I want them. The rifle pits are manned ready for a dawn attack and Apaches don't attack in the dark."

"They move in it," Ike answered. "Why don't you hustle all the women and kids along to the church there and get all the powder and shot from the store ready for when Lobo Colorado comes?"

"There'll be time for that when the attack comes."

In his heart Ellwood knew every word the miner said was true. The women and children should be at the church, behind the safety of those big walls, so should Millet's stock of firearms and ammunition. He'd tried to get the storekeeper to move that vital stock to safety, but Millet was shifty and evasive. There was a limit to what a town marshal could do. The limit was reached when it came to making a man do something like move his personal property. Without something more definite than they knew at the moment, Ellwood was helpless to make Millet do anything. The marshal would not allow these miners to see how helpless he was.

Zeke and Ike exchanged knowing looks as Ellwood turned to walk away. Ike let out an angry growl, and started forward but his friend caught his arm.

"Ain't no use nor need for it. He wouldn't listen to no low men like you. See he's read him a couple of them books about military tactics, like that officer boy we scouted for in the desert country. Allows it makes him an all-fired expert. He wouldn't listen to no common men like us, Ike. Got him a real bad shock coming."

"You fixing in to light for some place safe?"

"If I thought we could make it through Lobo Colorado's boys I'd say yes to that. But there ain't no such chance. I got me a feeling, Ike. They's all round us right now, and just waiting for dawn. Happen we left town we'd right soon be wishing we was back again."

They turned and lounged back towards the church. Crossing the plaza a low whistle came to their ears and brought them to an instant halt. Zeke whistled in reply before they moved on. Even so, a rifle was lined on them from the gate as they moved towards it and did not lower until the sentry knew for certain who they were.

"You see him?" asked the sentry.

"We saw him," agreed Zeke. "All the boys inside?"

"All but Walapai. Ole Winnie-Mae started to give out her Apache call, and he slipped out to make a scout."

Zeke nodded his approval of Walapai's actions. Every miner who kept the same burro for any length of time got to know the various ways it brayed and Winnie-Mae was Walapai's companion for many long years. The oldster was full capable of taking care of himself out there in the darkness. Walapai was a lone-wolf prospector when Lobo Colorado was a boy just starting on horse herding, and a man did not work alone for all those years in Apache country without learning to look after himself.

A small fire was burning by the protecting wall. Its flickering flames showing the faces of the miners as they gathered round it. All looked at Ike and Zeke with interest, for they knew what the two men attempted to do. They also knew, without being told, what the result was and none were surprised.

Before Zeke could say a word they heard a low whistle, replied to by the sentry and a few seconds after the short, whiskery shape of old Walapai slouched into the light of the fire. He was trailing his old Sharps rifle in one hand, the other held something which looked like a long black wig. Or would have to a man who'd never seen a fresh took, blood dripping Apache scalp.

Dropping to his haunches with the ease of a man who sat in a chair maybe once every three or four years, Walapai leaned his rifle against the wall. Dipping his now free hand into his pocket he took out a piece of coal black tobacco. He bit off a chew, munched for a moment, then sent a spurt of juice flying into the fire.

"Ole Winnie-Mae was right."

"They're out there, are they?" asked the youngest of the miners. "It couldn't just have been a stray scout for the main bunch?"

"Maybe he was, sonny," Walapai grunted. "Only he warn't alone. They're out there, all round the town or I miss my guess. Comes dawn the main bunch'll hit right down the trail, but there'll be a few left over to come for the sides and the back of the church."

The other men listened, knowing old Walapai was not making wild guesses. He'd been out to make a scout and would have done just that. The scalp in his hand told a story. There'd been no shooting, so Walapai's old bowie knife must have been in use.

The young miner looked up. He was a brash, cocky youngster in his first year as a miner and held his own ability in high esteem. "Did that brave tell you anything, Walapai?" he asked.

"Sure," replied Walapai, contempt so thick it could almost be cut with a knife. "We sat us down and b'iled a cup of tea, then talked. Right out there with maybe a dozen of his friends round us. Then after we talked, I ses real perlite like: 'Can I scalp ye?' and he ses, 'Sure, but do it easy like and stick me fust, so I don't feel it.'"

"Allow ye speak a mite of Apache, Walapai," Zeke put in gently as the laugh at Dick's expense died down.

"L'arned it when I was living with Mangus Colorado,

back afore the war. But them boys out there ain't talking, not even to each other.''

"You talked to that bownecked Yankee major, didn't you?" asked another man.

"Sure, but he wouldn't listen to us.''

"So this's how she lies to me," Ike took up from where Zeke ended. "We got two slim choices left. One, we heads for Fort Owen, and the pertection of the United States cavalry, what we pays taxes for. I reckon that might be just a leetle touch unhealthy as of what Senator Walapai just told us. Two, we stays on here, forts up the old church and does what we can to pertect ourselves.''

"Then this here council decides we stays on here?"

"Took and carried unanimous," agreed Ike.

"Put it that Zeke's in command," drawled Walapai. "All in favor?"

There was complete agreement with his words. The miners were as one in their vote on staying on, defending the church. Even one as hot-headed and inexperienced as young Dick knew the futility of trying to make a run for Fort Owen. They would be trapped by the encircling Apaches, or caught in the open and butchered. Here in the church, standing on the stone platform along the base of the wall, a man could fire over with little danger to himself. They would be able to make a fight of it in the church and possibly hold out until help came from Fort Owen.

The second business, electing Zeke as their leader, was a matter of form. He would be their leader only in as much as he would coordinate their efforts. The miners were like the Apaches in that they accepted a leader, yet would fight their own way. The leader could merely direct their efforts to the best and most useful end.

"We could use some more food," Zeke said thoughtfully.

"Shucks, we all got a week's supply, damn near," Dick objected. "That ought to last us."

"Sure, it'll last *us*," agreed Zeke. "But when the attack comes, there's going to be a lot of folks in here besides us. They won't be bringing any food with them."

"Where'd you reckon we could get food this time of the night?" asked Walapai. "I saw Haslett taking his missus to stay with the Millets for the night. Anyways, I can't see me paying out for food to give that bunch, and Haslett surely won't give his stock to us, not even to help out his friends."

"I reckon he might let us have it," Zeke replied, looking piously at the dark skies above. "Was we to go to his place and ask real perlite like. 'Special as he ain't there right now."

Walapai gave the harsh, coughing bark which served as a laugh in his book. "Ye wouldn't be suggesting that all us honest gents steals food from the store, now would you, Zeke? And me allus thinking you was such a clean living, sober and upright pillar of the church."

"Wouldn't call it stealing," said Zeke with a wide grin. "Not when he's been overcharging and underweighing us for years. And it'll be his friends who's eating the food."

The other men chuckled at the thought of Haslett's face when he found his food stocks were being eaten by his friends. The good citizens of Baptist's Hollow would be living on stolen food and would also be a good laugh.

"I reckon a couple of us should stay here," Walapai remarked. "Lobo Colorado ain't going to miss a chance to get a few of his boys inside the walls during the dark hours."

"Who'd you want with you?" Zeke asked, knowing Walapai was calling the play right. "Don't take too many, it'll need most of us to get the food here."

"Take young Dick if you like. Both me'n him having a good name to lose and not wanting to be mixed up with the robbery and sich."

Zeke gave his consent and the men prepared to take action. The fire was doused for a start. Then Zeke led all but Walapai and Dick out into the night, making for the Haslett store.

Walapai rose, making no attempt to pick up his rifle, and Dick followed him, leaving the Winchester which was his pride and joy behind. They went to the rear wall and Walapai grunted in satisfaction.

"Ain't none over yet. So we'll just settle down and listen a piece," he said.

"Sure," agreed Dick and dropped his hand to his side, loosening the Colt in his holster.

"Naw, Dick boy!" Walapai hissed. His hand caught Dick's wrist. "No guns. You got a knife with you?"

"Course I have!" Dick grunted and drew the eight-inch-bladed knife from the sheath at his right side.

"That thing? It'll have to do I reckon."

Dick looked down and could just make out the shape in Walapai's hand. It was the eleven-and-a-half-inch-long blade of the old timer's bowie knife. Walapai always carried his weapon with him, and Dick was inclined to scoff at it as being a piece of useless decoration. Now the scoffing was not in evidence, for Dick's own knife, sharp though it was, did not appear to be anything like the weapon a man would care to trust his life to.

The night was dark, the moon a mere sliver, and even the stars faded into almost nothing. There was nothing to be seen by the two men as they sat with their backs to the wall. Dick would much rather have been standing on the stone ramp and looking over the wall for some sign of the approaching, expected Apaches. He sat for a time without moving, the knife in his hand, eyes on the dull bulk of the church which loomed before him.

"I can't hear a thing for them damned crickets," he hissed after a time.

"Yeah, lovely sound, ain't it?" Walapai answered, holding his voice down as low as Dick's whisper. Then his hand tightened on Dick's sleeve, "*Listen!*"

Dick strained his ears to catch the sound which attracted Walapai's attention and brought the urgent hissed warning. He could hear nothing, not a sound of any kind. Even the crickets no longer chirped. By his side he sensed Walapai was standing and came to his feet, facing the wall. He did not know what to make of things and opened his mouth to whisper an inquiry. It was too late, Walapai had faded off into the blackness.

Some instinct made Dick look up. The wall rose black above him, the top of it making a darker slash against the dull sky. Straight and level the wall top ran. Dick gulped down something, his mouth suddenly going dry. The wall top above him was no longer straight and level. There was a bulge on it, a lump which was not there a few seconds before. Something was on top of the wall and swinging over.

A feeling of panic hit Dick, but he held his nerves in control. He realized what that shape was, even before it began to slide down the wall towards him. There were two other shapes on the wall top even as Dick lunged forward. He drove his knife forward and into the shape, feeling the point bite home and sink in. There was a gasping cry from the yielding thing as the knife sank home. At the same moment Dick heard a muffled rush of steps and a soggy thud. Then he felt a weight of the Apache coming down on him, falling backwards. His hand slipped from the sticky, wet hilt of his knife, and he staggered to fall. The hot, half-naked, sweaty body of the Apache landed on top of him.

Grappling with the Apache Dick struggled desperately throwing his arm around the bare throat, while his other hand struck wildly. Then he heard a sound which almost caused him to let go. It was a sound which would scare any man who heard it, a sound Dick knew well. Deep and harsh it rolled out in the darkness, the coughing, roaring snarl of an enraged grizzly bear. In desperation Dick rolled the Apache from him and was about to attack again when he saw the man was still. It struck Dick then that the Apache was dead, had been within a couple of seconds of the knife going home.

Dick came to his feet, hand fanning to his side, and found an empty holster; he had forgotten to refasten it. He was unarmed and there were Apaches in the church grounds. More, there was, or appeared to be, a mean old silvertip grizzly near at hand. He looked up. The top of the wall was suddenly straight and clear again. On the other side he thought he heard the gentle swish of fast-running feet. Then after a few minutes of silence, the crickets started their chirping again.

A hand gripped Dick's arm. He gave a yell and swung a wild fist, the yell came again as his knuckles hit the wall. The yelp of pain brought a low chuckle, and he made out that it was Walapai standing by his side.

"See you got one, boy," Walapai said, and his voice was the sweetest sound Dick ever remembered hearing. "Good, I got me another. Rest's gone now and they ain't likely to be back."

Dick sank to the ground, for suddenly his knees would no longer support his weight. Then he realized Walapai was talking in a normal voice and gasped. "What the hell was that growl? It sounded like a silvertip."

"Did, huh?" Walapai sounded just a little mite pleased. "I'll bet them Apaches thought it war, too."

"You did it?"

"Why sure. See Apaches think the silvertip's bad medicine. Allow the spirits of the bad folks go into silvertips when they die. Won't go within a country mile of a silvertip, won't any Apache. Good thing to remember, boy. Lost something?"

Dick was trying to find his revolver without Walapai noticing his folly. He heard a rasping sound, and the flickering light of a match showed him his gun. He went to pick up the Colt, and heard Walapai grunt. The old timer was bending over Dick's victim, and pulling out the knife.

"Waal I swan, boy." Walapai grunted as he came to Dick's side. "I wronged you and that little bitty knife of your'n. I never thought you could kill a man with it, I surely didn't."

Dick was pleased the darkness prevented Walapai seeing the flush of embarrassment which came to his face. All the time he'd been looking down on Walapai, thinking the big, wicked looking old bowie knife was a thing long out of date. At the same time Walapai must have been laughing at Dick's own knife as a toy unfit for the doing of any kind of man's work.

"Maybe they'll be back," remarked Dick, as he sheathed his knife and holstered the Colt.

"Tain't likely, boy. They'll allow their medicine's bad, us waiting for them and hearing a silvertip. They was only a small bunch. Knowed we was inside the church and snuck in the back way. Didn't aim to stay on here, we was too many for 'em."

"What'd they want then?"

"Kill one of our look-outs if they could. And leave this body down the well."

Dick gulped. A body down the well would ruin it, pollute the water. That was why the small bunch of Apaches came, not to take and hold the church until the other Apaches wipped out the town. It was a devilish plan and one well in keeping with the way the Apache fought.

"Maybe they'll be back, Walapai."

"Sure, but it ain't likely. We'll bide here just the same, until dawn. You can go fetch our rifles when the boys come back."

Dick was still straining his ears, trying to catch any slight sound from the other side of the wall, "Damn those crickets. I can't hear a thing for them."

"When you don't hear them it's time to start worrying," replied Walapai. "It means there's somebody coming when they stops singing out. Now me, I could stop here and listen to them singing all night."

"Tell you something, Walapai," Dick replied, sounding very sincere. "So could I. It's the sweetest sound I ever did hear."

The other miners made for the Haslett store. They did not know what was happening in the church, but all knew Walapai could take care of himself. Their own business was of more importance at the moment. Church Street was dark and deserted. Not a light showed. The rest of the town was not brightly lit either, but there were enough lights showing through curtained windows to indicate how few people were sleeping in Baptist's Hollow.

Zeke worked fast. He sent his men to keep watch, then went to the side window of the store and looked in. The building was dark and there was no sign of any life in it. With the Hasletts spending the night with the Millet family and their hired help having left that morning, there would be no one in the building. That was all to the good for Haslett would not take kindly to what the miners planned on doing. Even if he and his friends were the ones who would benefit by it.

Carefully Zeke put his old hat over his palm and began to push on the pane of glass. For a moment it held, then snapped and fell in with a slight tinkle. Inserting his hand, Zeke unfastened the window catch and lifted the protesting sash. He was about to slip in when one of the other men whispered:

"You done this sort of thing afore, Zeke. Sure the Pinkertons aren't looking for you?"

Zeke grinned and slipped in through the window, followed by Ike. They struck matches and went to work fast. A pile of sacks was found first. Then they began to fill each sack with food. They worked fast and took only the essential foods, for there was not much time. At midnight the guards at the rifle pits would be changed, and this must be done before that happened. There was a chance Haslett might come to the store on his way to the pits, but it was not likely. Zeke wanted to be finished before that happened.

With each sack filled it was passed out of the window,

and a miner would make a fast trip to the church with it. They used a small room at the rear of the building as a store, leaving one man on watch there and not disturbing Walapai.

Zeke and Ike took all they needed, enough food to keep the town supplied, on short rations, for almost a week. There was little left of Haslett's stock by the time they finished. A raid on the Haslett kitchen brought a limited supply of cooking utensils. Then the men left.

Back at the church they relit the small fire and settled down. Walapai joined them with word of the raid and praise for the way Dick handled himself. Then plans were made for the following morning. After that the miners settled down to sleep, stretching out on the hard ground. They took turns in watching and, as the first distant streaks of light showed in the east, rose.

"Soon be coming," Ike remarked.

Zeke nodded, it would soon be time. The attack would begin and all hell would break loose on the town of Baptist's Hollow.

CHAPTER NINE

Dawn at Baptist's Hollow

The sky was just faintly tinged with a fine, first red glow in the east. It was that first glow which, while not affecting the surrounding darkness, brought a warning that dawn was on hand.

Resting his rifle on the earth in front of his rifle pit, Major Ellwood tried to see through the blackness of the night around him. It appeared to him, as he strained to see something in the darkness, that the night was blacker now. In his pit he heard Haslett and Millet stirring and knew they were as awake and alert as only badly scared men could be. The other pits were manned ready, although it had been no easy task to stir the men out to relieve their friends. Ellwood did it in the end, making enemies of many people. Somehow he did not mind that. His time in the town was limited. The Town Council would never forgive him his action in making them take their fair share of the defense of the town and would have him out of his office as soon as they could. They did not worry him, he meant to leave Baptist's Hollow and make a fresh start in some other town.

Looking around him, even in the blackness, Ellwood could feel the tension and nervousness of the other men.

Soon they would know if Lobo Colorado planned to make his attack. It would be the moment of truth for many of them. Lobo Colorado was going to get the surprise of his life when he ran up against the rifle pits.

That was where Ellwood made his biggest mistake.

Lobo Colorado knew all about the rifle pits, had known almost as soon as they were begun. His men were watching the town and had been ever since Ramon went under. They moved in ready the day after the treacherous attack on their village, for this was to be the first town in Lobo Colorado's plan to sweep the white-eyes from the Apache lands for ever.

The chief did not know what those rifle pits were; the Army had never been foolish enough to use such things against a fast-moving, agile and vindictive fighter like the Apache, having learned their lesson against lesser tribes further east; he did know the tremendous disadvantage being in the pits was for the white-eyes. He made no move to stop their being dug or manned. They would be graves for the men who sat in them.

Even now his brave-heart warriors were moving in on the pits. Men slid forward along the ground, inching silently ever nearer, in the Apache way. With weapons held ready, they were closing in on those foolish white-eyes and by the time there was light to see by would be ready for their final rush. It would be a sudden, violent and spectacular move. The white-eyes would find themselves faced with a mass of yelling, shooting Apaches, would be smashed under, swarmed over in one wild rush. At the same moment smaller parties of men would be rushing on foot down the slopes on the other three sides of the town. Then, while panic and pandemonium reigned among the white-eyes, the main body of the Apache force, mounted and ready, would hurl themselves in through the open end of the Hollow.

It was a well-laid plan, one worthy of a great leader. It was a war plan such as the other Apache greats, Mangus Colorado, Cochise, Geronimo or Victorio made and put into operation with success.

So it was a pity that all Lobo Colorado's men were not veterans, battle-tried and found true in such a situation. One of the advancing party was a mere boy, a stripling fresh from horse-herding and newly initiated into his father's war lodge. The boy was wriggling forward with the older men, his old single-shot rifle held across his arms as he advanced. His eyes picked out the shape of the rifle pit ahead of him, making out the shape through the darkness.

This would be a great day for him, a day for doing deeds long to be boasted of in the wickiups. That he was sure of. He wriggled on faster than the other braves and drawing ahead of them, his head full of thoughts of how he would count many a coup this day.

Fifty yards from the pits the boy came to a halt, the whole of the creeping line freezing down like statues, hugging the earth and lying without a move. The boy watched the white-eye stand up in one of the foolish holes, an urge to kill came over the young Apache. It would be something for his father to sing over, at the great victory feast that night, how his son, in his first fight, killed the first white-eye. With that thought in mind, forgetting every order Lobo Colorado gave him, the youngest brought up his rifle and fired.

In the pits, the light getting better by the minute, there was a vague uneasy feeling that they'd been wasting their time. Haslett grunted his disgust and stood erect to try and get a better view around him. The storekeeper could see nothing and turned to say:

"There's nothing out there. I told you——!"

The rifle bullet ripped Millet's hat from his head, sending it spinning to one side. With a howl of fear Millet went back into the hole like a gopher hunting cover. Even as he dropped every Apache came up, screaming out their wild war yells, and charged.

The men in the pits were taken completely by surprise and that very surprise saved them from being trampled under in that first rush. Every man held a loaded, cocked rifle, finger on trigger. In a purely involuntary move every finger tightened, and the resulting volley sounded like a crack from a well-trained troop of cavalry. What it lacked in accuracy the volley made up in sound. Five Apaches went rolling in the dust, and the rest hesitated. Ellwood tried to press his advantage by control volley firing, but there was no controling those scared men in the pits. The only good thing was that each of them, in his panic, kept up a rapid, if mostly wild, fire. The sheer volume of fire brought the Apache attack to a halt, sending the warriors dropping flat to the ground. The attacking party just seemed to disappear, fading down into the soil and going out of sight.

Beyond the rim Lobo Colorado heard the first shot, then the roaring volley, followed by the rapid crash of fire. The chief did not own and would not have known how to use a watch, but he was a fair judge of time. When he heard the first shot he knew something was bad wrong. One shot must mean that one of his men had been seen and the surprise attack brought up short.

Jumping his big horse to the head of the slope Lobo Colorado looked down and saw his men going into the ground. It was fast getting light now, and he could see all which happened below. He knew he must bring his other force in before he wanted to. Swinging around on his horse's back he let out a wild, ringing war yell which brought the mounted Apaches pouring forward, up slope, on to the stage trail, and down towards the rifle pits.

When Ellwood's men saw the Apaches hit the ground and start back up the slope they thought things were over. They heard the wild yell which started the foot Apaches moving back and began to cheer. Haslett lifted his face from the ground where he'd kept it since nearly getting shot, looked at Millet and asked what was happening.

"We've got 'em licked!" Millet howled in delight. "We've licked 'em——!"

The words came to an abrupt end, and Millet's fat face lost all the florid color it had originally showed, his eyes bulged out at what he saw. A mass of mounted Apaches came into view on the stage trail, and with a wild ringing roar of war-shouts sent their horses hurling forward.

Half a second ahead of the others, Millet saw what the miners knew all along. The rifle pits were a death trap when faced with the onrush of cavalry. He knew they had no chance. That was when Millet lost his head. In a wild panic he threw aside his rifle, clawed out of the hole and ran for it. Haslett, as befitting a leading citizen of the town, was next to go, dropping his Winchester and making good time in his dash for town. The panic was infectious, man after man leapt from the pits and ran for the safety of the town.

Ellwood saw his men running and with the four who remained firm tried to fight a rearguard action. They fired fast, and their fire held back the braves for a few vital seconds, allowing them to start backing off for the town.

In the town, even as the first shot was fired, the miners were ready. They split into four parties, Walapai with three men to hold the rear wall of the church. Ike took three men to defend the left flank of the town, four more going to the right. Zeke, with the other four headed as fast as they could along Church Street to give what help they could to the men in the rifle pits. By the time they were passing the last building, they heard the steady crash of shots all round the town and knew the big attack was on.

Zeke brought his men to a halt by the final building of the town, their rifle fire directed with accuracy on the attacking braves. Millet raced by them, sprinting along at a speed which was surprising in one of his bulk. Behind him came the other men, running with the fear of death on them, only a few had even brought their weapons with them.

It was only the arrival and straight shooting of Zeke's party which saved Ellwood's life. His backers were all down, and he fought a desperate covering action to try and hold back the charging Apaches. The rapid fire of five men who could lay a rifle and call down their shots brought confusion to the attackers, but it was only a temporary confusion. Zeke and his men all knew it. Behind them all was confusion and pandemonium as women, children and such men who were not in the rifle pits streamed from the homes. There was a rush for the church, a few, a very few, men stayed on to help the miners, or came to back up Zeke and the group at the end of Church Street.

The Apaches who made their attack on foot were back to their horses now. On the rim Lobo Colorado saw his first party of horsemen milling under the rapid fire of the five accurate rifles. Throwing back his head

Lobo Colorado brought out a shout from his deep barrel of a chest. It was a shout which carried to the men on the edge of town. Zeke spoke Apache, and the words brought the hair standing bristly and stiff along the back of his neck.

"Brave up, brothers!" Lobo Colorado's booming shout rang out over every other sound. "This is a good day to die!"

It was a shout no self-respecting Apache brave could resist. Not when their great war chief was hurling his horse down the slope towards them. The braves sent their horses leaping forward, hurling down the slope to count coup, to loot, to kill.

Ellwood stopped by Zeke's side, rubbing the blood from his face and then forced bullets into the breach of his Winchester. The old miner was cooly firing at the Apaches, working as fast as he could to reload the old Remington rifle. He hoped for a clear shot at Lobo Colorado but did not get the chance. Glancing sideways at Ellwood, he growled:

"Reckon this's where we go dead, Major. Head for the church!"

Zeke and his men, except the two who would not be coming, backed off, their steady volley firing slowing the charge of the Apaches. Then Zeke gave a grunt of pain and dropped, a bullet through his leg. Ellwood bent, helped Zeke up, got him across his shoulders and tried to lift the rifle.

"Head for the church with Zeke, Major," a miner gasped out. "We'll do what we can to stop them."

Ellwood did not hesitate, he turned and ran for it, carrying the wounded man across his shoulders. He went by the jail, ignoring the scared yells of the two prisoners, making for the church to leave Zeke and return to help the remaining miners.

It was at this moment Dusty Fog brought his party into the attack, coming in behind the charging Apaches. They came from the stage trail and down the slope towards the town, a charging, shooting, wild yelling body of men with the wagons rocking and swaying in the center of the bunch. They smashed into the Apaches from behind, the attack coming as a complete surprise.

It was a brief, hectic madhouse as guns roared, horses squealed, men shouted and cursed. Through it all, even in the wild rush Dusty could find time to admire the superb horsemanship of the Apaches as they wheeled and turned their light war-ponies before the heavier cavalry mounts.

Bogran came boiling up in the churned-up dust behind Dusty. He saw the small Texan ahead and a light of hatred came over his face. This was his chance to avenge himself on the man who beat and humiliated him. Bringing up his revolver he lined it on Dusty's back, then drew back the hammer. Then he stiffened, a piece of the front of his tunic erupted in a bloody mess and slowly he keeled out of the saddle. Harris, the prisoner, came by, levering a fresh bullet into the chamber of the Springfield carbine. He looked down as his horse went by Bogran's back-shot body.

"You won't abuse no more prisoners, Bogran," he hissed, "nor shoot a good man in the back either."

Dusty Fog would never know how close he came to death, or that he owed his life to a man who was going to the Stockade for life.

Dusty saw a painted, screaming warrior ahead of him. There was no time to do anything but send the huge paint smashing into the war-pony and hope for the best. Down went the little Apache horse, and Dusty's right hand Colt wrote a finish to the warrior.

Then they were through the Apaches, but their trouble was only just beginning. Lobo Colorado's men were taken by surprise by the sudden and unexpected attack from behind. They broke and scattered, not knowing for sure how many men were in the attacking party. Now they knew and could figure odds of over ten to one being good medicine. They were reforming and preparing to come on Dusty and his men like a pack of wolves on a hamstrung buffalo.

"Fight on foot!" Dusty roared. "Waco, three men to run the horses to the church."

Waco waved a hand in answer to the order, although he did not wish to leave his friends in the middle of a good fight. He and the three men Dusty allocated the task of handling the horses closed in and headed them for the church, heading along the now almost deserted Church Street. Behind him, on foot, the men ranged alongside the startled miners, and Dusty's voice shouted an order for volley firing.

The first volley crashed out as Waco was approaching the jail, he heard a yell and looked at the barred cell window. To his amazement, two scared-looking faces peered out at him. It didn't take a mind-reading Comanche witch-woman to know what the two men wanted, or what had happened. It also took Waco less than half a second to go into action. He yelled to the men to keep on and swung his horse, leaving the saddle at a fast run. The big paint was headed on with the rest of the horses and Waco lit down on the sidewalk, went across it and tried the jail door. The door was locked and Waco wasted no time in thinking of right of property. His right foot came up and smashed into the side of the lock. The door held for the first kick, then burst open on the second, and Waco went in fast.

At the desk he halted a moment, his eyes going first to the prisoners, then to the chained, locked, line of rifles and shotguns on the wall rack. He let out a low snarled curse at what he saw. The town marshal must be a callous brute to leave prisoners locked in a cell at a time like this. He was worse than a brute to leave a line of weapons where they could fall into Apache hands.

Waco forgot the prisoners for a moment, the weapons were of more importance to him. He went and looked at the chain, then at the lock, this was big, strong and would take some breaking. There was no time to look for keys and a bullet was always an uncertain thing to break a lock with. There was always the more than even chance, if a bullet was tried, of jamming the lock completely and that would be fatal. There was not time to try and break the lock, not with Dusty and his men fighting a rear-guard action and being forced back along Church Street.

"Young man!" Scully's voice held an urgent note. "I am not averse to shuffling off this mortal coil—but I'd rather not do it today."

Waco tore his attention from the weapons on the wall and asked, "Where's the keys to the cell?"

"There's a set in the desk drawer," replied Scully. "The top drawer."

Moving fast Waco went to the desk, half expecting the drawer to be locked. It was not and he lifted out the key ring, crossed to the cell door and picked the most likely key to open the lock. It did not take more than twenty seconds, but they were the longest twenty seconds Scully could ever remember. There was a look of relief on his face as the cell door opened and he could get out. Followed by Willy, Scully went to the desk and pulled open the cupboard door at the side, from it he took his shoulder holster with the short barreled Colt Storekeeper revolver in it. He checked the revolver was still loaded, then handed Willy the old cap and ball Remington which the young man could use with some skill.

Waco stood looking at the line of weapons on the wall. He shook his head, they could not allow the rifles to fall into the Apache hands. The braves would have time in plenty to smash the lock, or break the chain and would so obtain Winchester rifles. There was only one thing Waco could do about it.

The matched, staghorn butted guns came from his holsters in a flickering blur of movement, then began to roar. Left and right Waco shot, throwing his lead with accuracy at the rifles. He aimed for the breeches of the rifles, knowing that a two hundred and eighty grain bullet would put the rifles out of action. By the time his guns were empty Waco knew there was not one weapon in that rack which would be of any use to the Apaches.

Dusty and his party were at the edge of the plaza by this time. It was the most dangerous part of the whole business. The crossing of that open space would be deadly dangerous.

"Lon, Chet!" Dusty yelled. "Half the men across the plaza and into the church, then give covering fire to the rest."

The two men moved fast, so did the men who Dusty selected as their party the previous night. Dusty held the rest, no longer volley firing but allowing the men to pick their own targets and fire at random. They made a stand at the end of Church Street, holding back the Apaches until the Ysabel Kid's wild Comanche scalp-yell rang out.

"Run for it!" Dusty yelled.

The soldiers and miners ran for the safety of the church. Then Dusty, Mark and Waco came last of all. They held their ground, allowing the other men to get halfway across the plaza, then turned and followed.

At the church, standing on the wall ramp on either side of the gate, the Ysabel Kid and Bronson worked their rifles like men possessed. They poured a stream of rapid and accurately thrown lead over their running friends and at the Apaches. Not one of the Apaches could show himself for long enough to take a careful aim at the three Texans, not when faced with two men who could call down their shots with such accuracy. To try to do so meant either death, or so near a miss that the aim was spoiled.

"What the hell happened?" Dusty snapped, as he came through the gate and drew to one side to face Ellwood.

"They were all over us," Ellwood answered, watching Dusty rest one revolver on the wall ramp while he re-loaded the other. "They just appeared from out of the ground. Millet and the others wouldn't stay and fight. I couldn't hold the rifle pits."

"Rifle pits!" Dusty spat the words out, seething with anger at the other man's mistakes. He'd seen the holes in passing, but never connected them with rifle pits. "You mean you tried to fight *Apaches* from those things?"

Before Ellwood could make any reply there was an interruption. Waco and Mark were standing by their friend, and Magoon came up to make his report. He'd been in the first party across the square, under orders to check on the defenses of the church as soon as he reached it. His report was anything but satisfactory.

"We lost nine men, including Bogran and both Stockade corporals. Used up a fair piece of ammunition. Got four walking wounded."

"That figures," Dusty replied. "Mark, you and Paddy make the rounds, find out how much ammunition each man's got. How's your supply, Marshal?"

"Supply?" Ellwood repeated, shaking his head as if to clear it. "We've no supply other than what we've got with us."

It took Dusty just half a second to get the implication of the words. He could hardly believe that the marshal had failed to collect the hardware store stock.

"How about the stuff from the hardware store?" growled Mark. "Or does the owner expect us to buy it from him?"

"The hardware store?" Ellwood gasped, then his face lost all its color. "We didn't bring the stock from the store last night. There was no certainty that the Apaches would attack, and I couldn't make Millet move his private property. So we never——"

"Damn it to hell, man!" Dusty's voice dropped to an angry hiss. "You surely cleared the ammunition and arms out of the store, didn't you?"

"No!" Ellwood's reply was no louder than Dusty's question. Suddenly Ellwood knew the terrible consequences of his failure to take proper command and take the necessary precautions. In this time of need, he'd been found wanting in almost everything he'd done. "We thought there'd be time——"

Dusty was no longer listening. His face was set hard and grim as he turned to Magoon. "Tell off ten men. See they've all got a revolver full loaded and that they can handle it. Ten men, not including you."

Magoon went fast to obey. There was no time for

arguing, or for asking to be cut in on whatever Dusty planned. He knew most of the men and picked out the ten best revolver shots. Harris was one of the group. The man's face looked different somehow, since having got into action. He still held the Springfield carbine but was also in possession of a revolver, taken from one of the men killed on the street. He moved forward fast, not knowing what his duty was to be but ready to go along with the small Texan's orders.

The ten men stood in a group by the gate, faced by the four Texans. Dusty looked them over and nodded his approval.

"All right," Dusty said, his voice quiet, yet every man of them heard it over the shooting from the walls. "There's powder, ammunition and weapons been left in the hardware store along the street. We can't allow them to fall into Apache hands, so we're going to bring out what we can and destroy the rest."

"Sounds risky," Harris grunted.

Dusty grinned back, recognizing the man's type. "You could be right." Then his eyes went to the Kid and Waco, "Nope," he said.

"Something wrong?" asked Waco innocently.

"Sure. You are. You're staying here to help Magoon. Lon, you and Chet get up in that bell tower with your rifles and start shooting. I'll send you some more men as soon as I can. I'll hear what you've got to tell me when I get back, Lon."

The Ysabel Kid did not argue, but Waco looked annoyed. Dusty was going into danger, and Waco thought he should be alongside his friend.

"Hell Dusty——!" Waco began.

Mark's big right hand gripped Waco's shoulder, the powerful fingers in hard and causing Waco, no weakling himself, to wince in pain. Mark's eyes went to Waco's face, and he snapped, "You do as you're told, boy. There's not the time to argue about it."

"Time we went," Dusty said, then he gripped Waco's hand, a smile playing on his lips. "Look, boy. Happen Mark and I don't make it, the bank draft's in my warbag. You and Lon take it to Colonel Raines, get the hosses and take them to Uncle Devil—and see you get good stock."

Waco did not trust himself to reply. He turned and went to where his horse stood with the others, pulled the Winchester from his saddleboot and came back to leap on the ramp and line the rifle over the wall. His face was hard, cold, set and grim as he looked at the men along the wall from him.

"Put down two volleys, boy," Dusty called. "Then we'll make a run for it."

"Make every shot count," Mark went on.

Twice came the crashing roar of a volley, the lead slashing at the Apaches across the plaza. Then, guns in hand, Dusty and his party went through the open gate and sprinted for the other side of the open square, for Church Street and the Millet hardware store.

CHAPTER TEN

Death of a Drunken Goldbrick

Luck favored Dusty's party as they charged across the square. Lobo Colorado was still out of town, making his medicine, and the other braves knew it would take some time for them to get the white-eyes out of the church. There was no great rush, the white-eyes were not going any place for a spell, and the town lay empty, inviting all braves to go and help themselves to loot. The Wells Fargo corral and the livery barn were the prime objectives, the horses herded off out of town. Then the houses at the other side of the town were invaded by eager braves, taking what they wanted and smashing anything they did not. Lobo Colorado's medicine was good. They'd taken the town, would soon kill all the white-eyes. Right now there was much loot to be gathered. The squaws would think highly of the braves when they saw it.

Consequently, Dusty and his men did not meet up with much opposition as they went across the square. Only a few young hot-heads remained to oppose them, and in the face of a determined charge, backed by the rifle fire from the bell tower, they backed off. Once Dusty's party reached Church Street, they met with some stiffer opposition from Apaches who were looting in the saloon and Wells Fargo office.

Dusty saw an Apache appear at the upstairs window of a house, rifle slanting down. The Colt in Dusty's left hand appeared to line of its own accord, roaring out once, and the Apache crashed through the window to land on the sidewalk. At the same moment Mark cut down on a brave who came through the batwing doors of the saloon, revolver in one hand, bottle of whisky in the other. A third brave was lining his rifle on the advancing white men when he spun around and went rolling in the dirt. Up in the bell tower the Ysabel Kid levered another bullet into his smoking rifle and looked for a fresh target.

Dusty's party was at the hardware store now, and Mark hurled himself up, across the sidewalk, his shoulder ramming into the store's door. Millet was proud of the strength of his household fittings, but that door burst open under Mark's crashing weight, splintering open as if it were matchwood. Before the men could make the comparative safety of the store, one of their number went down, headtop torn away by a soft lead muzzle-loader ball. Harris gave a grunt of pain as lead caught him. He stumbled but Dusty shoved away one Colt, caught him and helped him through the door.

"Get to it!" Dusty snapped, lowered Harris into a chair and looked at the blood which oozed from between the man's fingers as he held the hole in his stomach. "You three watch the windows, rest of you set to and load those rifles. Make sure the barrels aren't clogged with grease before you try and use them. Same with the revolvers. Take what you can carry, load them and bust the rest." He turned to the wounded man, "I'll see what I can do for you."

Harris's laugh was harsh and grating. "Don't bother none, Captain. I'm done, gutshot. How the hell do you reckon I'll make it back to the church?"

Dusty could see that the wound in these circumstances was fatal. The bullet caught Harris in the stomach, and there was no hope of medical aid for him. There was no way they could take him back to the church with them. Even without the danger of the Apaches and the men all carrying a load of arms and ammunition, there was nothing but danger in moving a man as badly hurt as this one. Like Harris said, there was nothing they could do for him.

One thing Dusty knew for sure. He could not leave Harris to fall into the Apache hands. Not alive at any rate. That was a problem Dusty would have to face when the time for departure came.

Right now there was too much to do to worry about when the time came for them to leave. He watched the three men at the windows, they were firing steadily at the lean, lithe, dark shapes which flitted into position around the building. The Apache braves knew what this store sold and knew why the white-eyes were inside. They would do all they could to prevent the arms being taken out.

"Going to be a mite dangerous, Dusty," Mark said as he joined his friend by the counter. "Give me first choice at the remuda and I'd take being back home to the O.D. Connected right now."

"So would I," agreed Dusty and looked around the room. "Where the hell does he store his ammunition and powder?"

"Behind the counter——" Harris gasped. "Got him a trapdoor leads into a cellar. I saw him go down it one time when I called in, riding courier."

Dusty and Mark went over the counter and looked down at the padlocked trapdoor leading into the cellar. Mark grunted and called to one of the soldiers to hand him a crowbar from the pile in the corner. It might have been quicker to try and break the lock with a bullet —but not with the possibility of the bullet missing and ending up in a keg of gunpowder.

Taking the bar Mark inserted the end into the ring of the lock, then began to strain upwards. The lock was strong and held for a moment. Mark's giant muscles bunched and rolled until they almost looked as if they would rip his shirt. Then the lock snapped open, and Mark bent to jerk the trapdoor up. There was a small lamp under the counter. Dusty took and lit it, then led the way down the wooden steps. At the foot he looked around the small store room. Most conspicuous thing of all was a big barrel, the top of which was open. He went to the barrel and looked inside, it was as Dusty feared. In his attempts to prevent anyone stealing any of his gunpowder, Millet emptied the smaller kegs into one large barrel. This was three-quarter full and probably nailed to the floor as an added measure of safety. On the shelves were three boxes of bullets for either the .45 Colt or the .44.40 Winchester. An open wooden box next to the ammunition contained sticks of dynamite, but there was no sign of fuse or detonator. That figured, a man did not mix the two together if he could help it.

Mark went to the barrel and looked inside. He did not think the black grains were soot, or even fine ground charcoal.

"More than three-quarters full," he growled. "That damned, stupid nogood——"

"Cursing won't help us any, Mark," answered Dusty. "We can't tote this barrel out with us and it wouldn't be healthy to try and take the powder out in sacks. We'll just have to blow it up. Pass the ammunition boxes out to the men.''

Mark picked up the three boxes and shoved them up over the edge of the trapdoor on to the shop floor. Then he looked around the cellar and shook his head. "I can't see any fuses.''

"There aren't any," Dusty answered, and something in his voice made Mark look hard at him. "No chance of laying a powder trail down the steps either. Get the men out of here and head for the church, Mark. I'll give you five minutes start.''

Mark was long used to Dusty's cold courage, but the quietly spoken words shook him. "Like hell. You can handle the defense of the church better than I can. I'll be the one who——''

Dusty shook his head. He could not, would not, leave his friend to die. "It's my chore, Mark. I can't leave another man to do it.''

Without their knowing, the words carried to the ears of Harris. The wounded man sat hunched up in the chair and listened, then gritting his teeth forced himself on to his feet and edged around the counter to look down into the hole.

"Hey, you pair," his growled out words showed the pain he was in, "It's long gone time you was getting out of here.''

"It's not that easy," replied Dusty. "We can't leave this stuff here for the Apaches, and there's no fuse to set it off.''

"That so?" Harris grunted, then gritting his teeth he started to climb down the steps.

Mark guessed what was on the man's mind and helped him down. Harris swayed forward to lean on the top of the keg and look in. Dusty frowned, the man should be sitting down, not moving about with a wound like that. He opened his mouth to say something but Harris gave him no chance.

"Looks bad, real bad. Got a smoke, Cap'n?"

"*Smoke!* Down here?" Dusty snapped. "Have you gone loco or something?"

"If you're scared you can always get out," replied Harris, then he coughed and a trickle of blood ran down his chin. "Go on, roll me a smoke, leave me some matches—and get the hell out of here."

For a moment Dusty did not speak but from the sound of the heavier firing above knew the Apaches were pressing home a stronger attack. Then he shook his head:

"I can't ask a man to stay down here. I can't leave you——"

"And you can't take me with you," Harris interrupted. "I'm gutshot, and I'd not make it halfway to the church, not the way you'd have to carry me. Every man up in the store's loaded down, so how the hell are you going to manage me. You wouldn't have a chance with me along. Don't even like your chances without me."

"You can't ask me to stand by while you blow yourself up!"

"Why not, you aimed to stay here and do it."

"It's my duty to stay," replied Dusty. "And my place."

"Your place 'n' duty's down there at that church," Harris growled, grinning mirthlessly. "That's good, me telling a man like you what his duty is. Look, Cap'n, I'm hit bad. Even if I pull through, which ain't likely, I've got a life in the Stockade ahead of me, and you'd see I got there. You might not like doing it, but that wouldn't stop you. I know you Southern gentlemen. I reckon I'm getting off easy. Now get the hell out of here before I start in to crying on your shoulder."

Mark was hand-rolling a cigarette, working fast, with fingers which almost appeared to see. He licked the paper, whirled the finished smoke between his fingers and gave it to Harris. Then he turned to Dusty and his voice was low:

"He's right. You're needed at the church. Those folks need a leader and that town marshal isn't the man for it. He'll get them all killed. There's only you can pull them through."

Dusty did not reply. This was one of the hardest decisions he'd ever had to make. He watched Harris leaning on the keg and gritting his teeth, trying to hold on to consciousness. Dusty crew in a deep breath, then let it out again.

"Pass a chair down here," he raised his voice. "Move it."

There was time for Dusty and Mark to replenish the loads in their guns before the chair was passed down by a soldier. His face showed some worry and he said:

"There's a helluva lot of them out there, Cap'n. All got rifles and they ain't waiting to pass the time of day."

"Never thought they were," Dusty replied. "We'll need that dynamite, Mark."

"There's no fuses for it," Mark replied. "I surely hope we can find some."

Dusty hardly heard what his friend was saying. He turned to Harris. "Thanks, friend. Are there any messages for anybody?"

"Sure," Harris answered, sinking into the chair and

resting his elbow on the top of the keg. "Tell the colonel——" The message to the colonel was unprintable and hide searing. "Now you get the hell out of it," Harris finished, taking the cigarette and matches from Mark's hand. "Don't worry none, I'll see she blows."

"I'm not worried about that," Dusty said and raised his hand in a respectful salute, then nodded to Mark. "Get going."

Mark went up the steps, carrying two bundles of dynamite. He paused at the top and looked back at Harris. "*Adios*, soldier."

"Good luck," Harris grunted back. "I'd have liked to serve under you, Cap'n."

Dusty went to the store floor again. He found the men standing at the windows and pouring shots at the Apaches across the street. Dusty darted to the side of the open door and looked out. He could see things were not going to be easy. They'd be lucky if they got out of the store. There were some twenty or more Apaches on the other side of the street, in the building opposite or at the ends of it. All of the Apaches held rifles and were shooting back at the store. That door was a death trap. No man could get through it alive. Not with Apaches waiting for them. Apaches armed with repeating rifles.

"Hurry, damn you, hurry!" Harris's voice, sounding weak, came to Dusty's ears.

"Mark you, soldier!" Dusty snapped, indicating a grizzled old trooper who was nearest the door. "Take a bundle of dynamite each and stand on either side of the door. When I reach a count of three I want you to pitch the sticks at the Apaches. Lob them well up. The rest of you men pour on some lead against those Apaches. If you empty your gun drop it. All full loaded with ammunition?"

There was a mutter of agreement and the men started to shoot. They did not know what Dusty had in mind but all hoped he would get them out of the store. It was not the most safe place for a man to find himself and got even less safe by the second.

Mark knew what Dusty meant to try and do. It was a desperate chance, but it was all the chance they had left. They could not get out unless the rifles of the Apaches were stilled and the Indians confused. Everything depended on Dusty's skill with his matched guns, the skill which won him the Cochise Country Fair Pistol Shoot, the skill which made him a legend in his own lifetime.

"One," said Dusty, showing no more excitement than if he was about to perform some easy trick. "Two!" The two men drew back their arms and gauged the distance across to the Apaches. "Three!"

Mark and the soldier moved into the open space of the door, swinging their hands forward to send the bundles of dynamite flying into the air. Dusty held a gun in either hand, cocking them as he watched the flight of the bundles. He formed a picture of the flight, estimating where he need aim for bullet and bundle to meet. Then he brought up the right hand Colt and fired in a fast move which hardly appeared to wait for his taking aim.

The roar of the explosion drowned the bellow of the Colt. There was a brilliant flash. Almost instantly there sounded a second dull roar as the concussion of the first explosion detonated the second bundle.

Even without being packed into solid earth and building up the full explosive power through the packing, the dynamite gave a satisfactory result. The blast of the explosions came rushing down on to the Apaches at the other side of the street. It struck down on them,

leaving those nearest in shattered, bloody pulp and
throwing the others right off balance. The braves were
in no condition to prevent Dusty and his party leaving
the door.

Dusty and the other men had flattened down as soon
as he shot. Now they were up on their feet and Dusty
roared, ''Run for it! *Adios*, Harris!''

''Good luck, Cap'n,'' Harris called back, weak but
still defiant.

The soldiers, each one loaded down with ammunition
and weapons, left the store on the run. Dusty and Mark
were the last to leave, their guns out as they prepared to
fight their way back to the church. Only the Apaches
who'd been facing the hardware store were affected by
the explosion. There were many more on hand.

Standing on the wall of the church grounds, Waco
could see all that was happening along the street. He
saw Dusty and Mark fighting their way back towards
the church and knew how slight their chance of doing so
was. There were more Apaches moving in all the time,
flitting towards the sound of shooting.

Waco turned to Magoon, his eyes blazing. ''They
don't have a chance on foot. I'm taking horses to
them.''

''Boy's right,'' growled a miner. ''I'm with you,
Texas.''

Waco leaned his rifle against the wall and bounded to
the ground. He hit down running, eight soldiers and
miners following him. The young Texan did not waste
any time in the finer refinements of horse-mounting,
like placing his foot in the stirrup irons. He went up into
the saddle of that seventeen hand stallion in a single
bound, scooped up the reins and put his Kelly pet-
makers to work. The huge horse went forward in a leap-

ing bound, the eight other riders following. Waco went through the open gates and at the Apaches like a bat out of hell. The other men rode fast, but they could not keep up with the wild-eyed Texas boy.

Like a raging devil, his guns out and snarling, Waco tore across the plaza and on to Church Street. He rode like a centaur and shot like a fiend, tearing at the Apaches and along Church Street towards his friends. Waco's plan was simple. He was going to save his two friends or die trying. If Dusty Fog was going to be killed, Waco aimed to die by his side.

Dusty saw what was happening and swore that, at the first opportunity, he would take that blond heller and beat some sense of discipline into him. Waco should have stayed in the church where he would have been safe, not charged out on to the street and risk being killed.

The horsemen scattered the gathering Apaches and tore along the street. Waco brought his paint to a rump-scraping, sliding halt and was swinging the big horse in a tight circle even as he reached down a hand to Dusty. He'd holstered one gun ready for this, and catching Dusty's hand, swung him up behind the saddle of the paint. There was a sheepish grin on Waco's face, as he saw the look Dusty gave him.

"Never was no hand at choosing hosses," Waco said cheerily as Dusty settled down behind him. "And I sure didn't want to do it with Ole Devil waiting at the other end to look 'em over."

Dusty swung around, twisting on the back of the horse, to make sure all his remaining men were mounted. He saw a miner slide from his horse, then a soldier, the veteran who threw the dynamite, slump off the horse he'd mounted. The rest were all mounted now, and nothing could be gained by delaying their departure.

"Let's go!" Dusty yelled.

At his shout the horses were running, carrying double, but still making good time. Three more were shot down before they tore across the plaza and through the open gates of the church.

Dusty and his men came into the church grounds to the sound of cheering from the watching defenders. Every man, even those who lived in Baptist's Hollow, knew what that gallant group attempted to do. The cheers came from the heart, even Millet lifting his voice in them, although he was secretly wondering if he could make the town pay for the ammunition at some later date.

Dusty was in no mood for either the cheering or the eager congratulations which were being showered on him from all sides. Of his party only Mark, himself and four soldiers made it back to the church. The small amount of ammunition they'd managed to bring would not go far.

Wild with excitement and delight at Dusty being safe, Magoon was by the small Texan's side and slapping his back. Then the big sergeant stopped, his face flushed with embarrassment at his lack of respect for Captain Fog. Dusty hardly heard a word of Magoon's spluttered apologies. He was looking back towards the store and waiting. The explosion should have come by now, he thought. Perhaps Harris collapsed and was unconscious. Perhaps the Apaches shot Harris without his having a chance of setting off the powder charge.

In the cellar Harris sat on the hard chair and listened to the noises above his head. He'd been able to guess what happened, from the two explosions, Dusty's shouted farewell, and the sound of running feet. Now he sat alone, a grin, mirthless as on the fleshless face of a skull, playing on his lips. His lower body was numb and without feeling but his head was clear and his hands steady as he lit the cigarette. The smoke felt good as he drew it into his lungs, the harsh tobacco biting at the back of his throat. He blew out smoke and relaxed, hand held over the open top of the barrel so that the glowing cigarette end would fall into the powder even if he collapsed. So he sat there, waiting for certain death, yet neither afraid nor worried by it.

Above his head Harris heard soft footfalls and drew on the cigarette once more, sucking in the smoke and watching the glowing tip. His eyes raised to the Apaches again.

One brave stood at the top of the steps, then drew his knife and started to move down. To kill an enemy with a rifle was to count coup but not counted as so great an honor as killing with a knife. So the young Apache moved in with his knife in hand, to take the life of this strange white-eye soldier who grinned at him as if welcoming death. On the floor of the cellar the young Apache tensed for a spring which would carry him on to the white man and allow the knife to sink home.

It was at that moment Harris threw the red, glowing cigarette into the barrel.

The thunderous roar of the explosion shook the town from end to end, smashing windows even as far as the church, flattening nearby buildings and sending a wave of blast rushing out in all directions. Where the Millet store was, now only a few smoking, shattered timbers and a large hole in the ground remained.

The blast of the explosion threw the Apaches into confusion, flung Lobo Colorado to the ground and almost brought the attack on the town to a close. He rose and called his messengers to him, then sent them to gather all men at the houses facing the plaza. He thought of launching a big, all-out attack on the church and regaining the hold his medicine appeared to be losing.

Dusty Fog stiffened into a military brace, as the explosion brought women and children running from the church. His face was set, hard, and fighting down expression. A man was dead, a brave man dead to prevent those stupidly left supplies from falling into the hands of the Apaches. Dusty hated the thought of leaving Harris to blow up the store in such a way. Hated it even though there was no way he could have brought the man back to safety.

The citizens of Baptist's Hollow stood in a fast talking, gesticulating bunch and the miners gathered near to where Dusty stood with Magoon, ready to take his orders.

"That explosion, Cap'n," said Magoon, knowing something was troubling Dusty. "Reckon you must have left a fuse to Millet's powder supply."

"Not exactly!" Dusty's voice was harsh. "Harris took lead on the way in, was hit in the stomach. He said he'd stay on and—I didn't want to leave him back there and I couldn't bring him back with me."

"You did the right thing, Cap'n," Magoon replied, seeing Dusty was worried and feeling badly about leaving Harris. "You couldn't have stayed behind, your place's here, running the defense."

"I know that, Paddy. It's just that I hate to leave a good man to die like that—and Harris was a good man."

"Asking your pardon, Cap'n," Magoon said, stiffen-

ing into a brace and reddening with embarrassment at
what he was going to do. "It's time you started to make
plans for the living. We've hit the Apaches hard, even if
it did cost plenty of lives. If it hadn't been for your
handling of things this place'd be wiped out by now. I
don't know of any man who could have handled things
better than you have. And there's damned few who
could have handled it anywhere near as well as you
have."

"Thank you, Paddy. Thank you," Dusty answered.
He shook his head and then, once more, he became the
keen, efficient man Magoon could always remember
him as being. "When you put in your report of this fight
I'd like you to commend the bravery of Private Harris.
See he gets a special mention, will you?"

"That I will, Cap'n. He might have been a trouble-
maker and a drunken gold-brick, but by the Lord
above, he died like a man."

"That's right, Sergeant Magoon," agreed Dusty.
"He died like a man."

A better epitaph Private Harris, drunk, brawler,
trouble-causer, killer and real brave man, would not
have wished for.

CHAPTER ELEVEN

Six Votes for Captain Fog

"All right, Sergeant Magoon," Dusty said, laying aside thoughts of Harris and starting to give his orders. "I'll have the men split into two——"

"Now hold hard there," Ellwood snapped as he and the citizens of Baptist's Hollow started to move forward. "We're grateful for what you've done but I'll take command now."

"We don't like the high-handed way you've been handling things," squawked Millet pompously.

Dusty's voice was mild and gentle as the first whisper of a Texas blue northern storm. There was no other sound in the church grounds and his words carried to a lot of interested people. "You don't huh? So you don't like the high-handed way I'm handling things?"

"We don't," Millet replied, waxing brave with the backing of the rest of the town. "This's our home and Major Ellwood's our town marshal. He——"

"He's the damned, stupid, callous fellow who left two prisoners locked in the cells and left a stand of rifles that the Apaches could have used against us," Waco began hotly, riled up by someone implying Dusty Fog couldn't do everything better than any other man. "He didn't even have sense enough to get the powder and arms out of the hardware store.''

Ellwood's face darkened in a mixture of anger and shame at the words. He knew every word Waco said was true. He'd meant to release Scully and Willy and meant to return to the jail as soon as he brought Zeke to the safety of the church. It was just that there had not been the time to do so. He'd been worse than stupid on the other thing, the moving of Millet's stock. His failure to do so cost men their lives. He opened his mouth to say something but Dusty spoke, bringing Waco's angry tirade to a halt.

''The boy's telling the truth. You and all your people were warned and you still left arms, ammunition, powder and stuff behind for the Apaches. The miners would've helped but I bet you were so bow-necked you wouldn't even listen to them. Then you try and fight cavalry from rifle pits and haven't the guts to hold them long enough to let your folks get to safety. Mister, this's your town all right and if it didn't mean stopping an Apache uprising I'd say the hell with you and pull out right now.''

''You blew up my store,'' snapped Millet.

''That's right, mister. I blew up your store,'' Dusty replied, voice throbbing with anger. Mark moved behind his friend, ready to grab him if Dusty started one of his sudden and deadly dangerous karate attacks. Mark knew Dusty well and could tell the rage which was building up inside his friend. If Millet said or did the wrong thing Dusty would strike in the deadly way Tommy Okasi taught him and the big man would be rolling in agony, if not in his death throes, on the ground.

''Mister,'' Dusty went on, ''I blew your store up and I

wish you'd been in it when it blew. I lost six good men trying to do something which could have been done in safety last night. You could have done it but you didn't. Or didn't you reckon the Apaches would bother with it after you'd locked up and run out?''

"Most all you say's true," Ellwood put in. "But the citizens think that I, as mayor and town marshal, should take command again.''

"Like hell!" Magoon bellowed. "Why you——"

"Hold it down, Sergeant!" Dusty barked out. "This's between me and the marshal.''

"Asking your pardon, Cap'n Fog.'' said Ike, the miner, stepping from where his friends were interested onlookers. "But it ain't for him or you to say at all. It's for us that's got to follow who's got to say——"

"What Ike there's trying to say, Cap'n," interrupted Walapai, moving forward to flank his friend. "Him not have an eddicated throat like, is that we've all seed the way you handled things and the way they was mishandled up 'til you arrived——"

"So us uneddicated 'uns," Ike cut in, "allows you're the man to lead us. But we'll stay true to the democratic principles of our great 'n' glorious country and put it to a vote.'' He dropped his hand to the worn butt of his Remington revolver, his eyes appearing to pick Millet's fat stomach as first target. "I call down six votes for Captain Fog.''

"Why, it's taking the Army vote you are, Cap'n darlin','' Magoon went on, rubbing the walnut grips of his long barrelled Colt Cavalry Peacemaker. "And any Army man who doesn't agree'll be policing the stables for the rest of the time he's enlisted.''

"Which same's corruption," a soldier drawled from the wall where he was standing watch. "But I goes along with it and votes down for Cap'n Fog.''

There sounded an ominous double click as Big Em eased back the hammers of her sawed-off twelve-gauge and put her deep contralto voice in: "Us freighters stand for Cap'n Fog and graft-free administration.''

"The show folks lay down solid for Captain Fog, even those under-age," Phyllis went on and raged herself alongside Big Em.

Scully swung from his place on the wall, his revolver hanging negligently in his right hand, eyes on the citizens of Baptist's Hollow and the town marshal who abandoned him to an almost certain death. "As a convicted person," he said, "I don't get a vote. But I'm taking one for all that. Captain Fog and better food in jails."

Ellwood listened to the way the voting was going and watched the faces of the voters. True his supporters out-numbered the others and in a truly democratic election could carry the day. They would get nowhere in attempting to point this out, for the only reliable fighting force was solidly aligned behind Dusty Fog.

All too well Ellwood knew his own failures in this business. His lack of positive action in the organizing of the defenses, in the matter of the hardware store, they were all against him. He knew if it was not for Dusty Fog's well timed charge the town would have been wiped out, every person in it either dead or wishing he were. Ellwood was sure that the town would never have been left in so poor a position of defense with Dusty Fog in command. There was only one thing to do right now, and Major Ellwood was still man enough to do it.

With this thought in mind Major Ellwood not only conceded defeat at the impromptu polls, he swung his own vote solidly behind the man opposing him.

"Majority rules, Millet," he said, "and I go along for Captain Fog."

Dusty was never a man to gloat if he won. He turned his attention to the serious business on hand. They were fairly safe in the church as long as their food and ammunition held out. The man who was headed for Fort Owen would get help, and a troop of cavalry would be on hand in time to help them before the Apaches could get in. With that thought Dusty began to organize the defense.

"Let's not waste any more time. How are we off for food?"

"Not bad," grinned Ike. "Got enough for a week if none of us eats much. Got it stored in the back room of the church, guarded by our good friend Zeke, bust-up leg and all."

Dusty could guess where the food came from, for Ellwood showed some surprise at the statement, and Haslett looked both puzzled and worried. He asked no questions and got on to the important details.

"Phyllis, you, your gals and Big Em are the only women to be allowed outside the church. You'll take charge of the food, and I want a meal cooking up as fast as you can. Lay chivalry aside for one time and feed the menfolks first. Allow for a week and share the food accordingly, Major, you see to it that your womenfolk all know what I've said. That way there'll be no arguing."

"Yo?" Ellwood found himself giving the automatic reply he'd heard so often from cavalrymen.

"Why should those women be in charge of the food?" Haslett whined.

"Because the cap'n said so," growled Magoon. "Now shut your mouth, darlin', or I'll be compelled to do it with a boot."

Which ended any further objections the good citizens of Baptist's Hollow might have thought of raising and allowed Dusty to carry on without interruption.

"Mark," Dusty went on, hardly noticing the interruption. "Split the party into two groups. You and Paddy take charge of one, the Major and Corporal Tolitski handle the other. Find the four best shots and send them up in the tower under Chet Bronson."

Dusty turned then to the Ysabel Kid. "How about it, Lon?" he said.

"Waal, I wasn't exactly taking much notice, way we come through them, but my herd count reads Lobo Colorado's got Mescaleros, Pintos, Tontos, few each of Minbrenos, Chiracauha and Coyeteros. Could have just a touch of White Mountain boys to help bring on the whole boiling. But like I say, I couldn't be sure on that last."

"Sounds like some from near on each tribe of the Apache nation," remarked Dusty. "How the hell did they get together so fast after the shooting?"

The Kid shook his head. "I'm only part Indian, Dusty. And I gave up trying to figure out Indian thinking when a Commanche witch-woman told me all about the Battle of the Lil Bighorn—the morning after it happened."

Dusty nodded. He'd seen and heard of other such examples. "What do you reckon Lobo Colorado'll try now?"

"Nothing for a spell. He's got us here safe enough. We can't go no place and he surely doesn't want to, not until he's been in here and talked some to us. So he's setting back and waiting for something. More men, maybe, or he could be making medicine, trying to figger a way to get at us. We hit him hard, cost him men and his medicine's likely shaken. He'll have to do something slick and fast, or the other tribes' bad-hats'll reckon his medicine's no good. They won't follow a leader who's lost his medicine."

Dusty knew he could rely on the Ysabel Kid's Indian-savvy to get them through. "Was you Lobo Colorado, how'd you get the folks out of here?"

"That ain't a fair question. I'm Comanche and we fight different from Apaches."

"Just make a try at guessing anyways."

"Like I say, I'm Comanche. I'd wait until dark, then hit. Apaches don't make war in the night, though they might try to get men in to poison the well. They'll may-be not try again today. Comes dawn they'll make their move, just like they did this morning."

"Could be safe until dawn then?" Mark asked.

"Could be——"

"Dusty, there's some more braves just come in. Been three fair-sized bunches arrived, now a small one. Look tolerable excited about something," Bronson's voice came floating down to them.

"Watch 'em, Chet!" Dusty called back. "And don't go to sparking with Miss Molly until that's over."

"You go to hell and fry there!" Bronson yelled, and the others did not know how he was blushing.

"Been thinking about it, Dusty," remarked the Kid. "Lobo Colorado don't know how we stand for shells, but he'll figure we aren't long on them. So he'll start to try and make us waste it by sending fast riding bunches in. It might cost him a few men, but it'll use up our supply fast enough."

At that moment Waco returned. For once his young face was not smiling and friendly. It was hard, cold and deadly serious. Dusty knew something was wrong, but the result was worse than he expected.

"It runs to about ten rounds apiece for the revolvers and about one magazine full each for the Winchesters. The Sharps rifles or the Remingtons have a mite more, but not much. Looks like there's not much powder left for the percussion guns and no lead to make fresh loads."

At that moment they heard the fast drumming of hooves and Bronson yelled, "Three braves coming along Church Street, Dusty, look tolerable excited."

Dusty and Mark turned and looked over the walls. There were buildings burning in the town and the smoke, whipped along by the wind, was in their faces. They saw the three young braves hurling towards the plaza. One was wearing an ill-fitting cavalry jacket and waving something that looked like a ball in his hand.

The three braves came hurling on to the plaza and for the church walls. Dusty and Mark did not intend shooting, for there was no chance of the three making a serious attack. The braves were just making a name, taunting the defenders and with the smoke stinging the eyes added to the speed they rode there was not much chance of hitting them.

A revolver cracked from the gate, another took it up and before Dusty could stop them several men were pouring, wasting valuable bullets in an attempt to hit the fast riding braves.

"Stop that shooting!" Dusty roared; the soldiers and miners held their fire at the words, but the townsmen continued to shoot wildly.

One brave slid from his horse but the other two were in close and riding fast. The brave in the cavalry coat threw the thing he carried over the wall, yelled a derisive insult, whirled his horse and rode back unscathed by the hail of lead.

All eyes went to the thing the Apache threw over the wall. The Ysabel Kid bent down and rolled the severed human head over. The features were twisted in an expression of agony and barely recognizable. The tawny hair, side whiskers and big moustache told the Kid all he wanted to know. He straightened up, his face hard, Comanche-mean mask and his voice a deep-throated Dog Soldier's grunt:

"That soldier you sent to the fort, Dusty—He didn't make it."

CHAPTER TWELVE

Big Em's Load

Dusty looked down at the head of his messenger, then lifted his eyes to Mark Counter's face. "Who started all the shooting?"

"I did," Millet said and turned pompously from his place, looking as if he expected praise for a good piece of work.

Dusty's scorn was plain. "I might have known!"

"We shot one!" Haslett went on delightedly.

"Sure. You got one," drawled Mark, but there was no pleasure in his voice. It was hopeless trying to explain to such men that they'd used up a large portion of their ammunition supply to kill one brave who was not even menacing the church. Mark turned back to Dusty, "It's all my fault. I should have kept them hawg-tied. I put them in my party and left them there so I could keep an eye on them."

There was no time for worrying over spent ammunition. Dusty did not blame his friend for what happened. He knew it was to be expected when dealing with men like Millet and Haslett.

"Dusty!" called Bronson. "Lobo Colorado's talking with those two who just came down. Looks all excited about something. He's calling the braves away from the houses, all except for a few to hold us down.''

"It'll be coming soon, Dusty," the Kid warned. "He's gone to make his medicine and when that's done we'll have us some shooting to do."

"We might hold off one attack," Dusty remarked. "But that'll use about every bullet we've got."

"What's this wagon carrying, do you reckon, Dusty?" Mark asked and indicated Big Em's wagon, standing at the gate. "Wouldn't be healthy if it's carrying explosives. Not when the shooting starts."

Dusty and Mark went to examine the wagon, while the Kid climbed on the stand to look over the wall. The two Texans looked the big Conestoga wagon over but could see nothing to help them guess what the cargo was.

"It's not down on the springs much," Dusty drawled. "Load's not heavy."

"Could be payroll," Mark guessed.

"Not likely, is it. The Army sends payrolls in fast coaches with a major in command and a fair-sized escort."

Mark took out his clasp-knife and opened the blade. "What say we have a little accident, Dusty?"

Dusty nodded. His friend cut the ropes which held the tarpaulin cover down. He raised the tarp slightly, and Dusty looked in underneath it. There was some light but not enough to allow Dusty to see much of what the wagon carried. He forced the tarp up and swung underneath it to stand in the wagon. Striking a match he looked at the cargo. Near to him were two long, rectangular boxes, one larger than the other. Behind these were two large, square boxes and other smaller square boxes which looked familiar in shape and form.

One thing Dusty did know was that the Army were not eager for the contents of the boxes to be known. All identifiable lettering on the boxes had been obliterated. Not just painted over but planed out of the wood. Dusty went to the larger of the rectangular boxes and bent over it. The match burned his fingers and he blew it out, then lit another. There was no mark of any kind on the box, or on the next he looked at. He was about to call on Mark for a crowbar and find out what was inside when he decided to look at the bigger square boxes.

The wood was planed down as on the others, but Dusty saw the work was not so well done as on the others. There was a faint outline left on one box and Dusty bent forward to examine it closer. He lit another match and felt the excitement hit him at the faint outline of what seemed to be a horse standing on its rear legs, forelegs pawing the air and what appeared to be a stick between the legs and a second in its mouth.

Dusty knew what that sign meant. He'd seen it often enough. It was the mark of the Colt Patent Firearms Manufacturing Company, the sign of the rampant colt. For all that Dusty held down his excitement. Colt was interested in other things besides firearms and there was no point in raising hopes to have them dashed again if this proved to be some other item, not weapons.

"Pass me that bar from the side of the wagon, Mark," said Dusty, trying to act and sound nonchalant.

"What is it?" asked Mark, bringing the bar and climbing under the canopy. He knew Dusty too well to be fooled by any amount of nonchalant acting.

Dusty did not reply. He worked the prongs of the bar under the lid of the big box and pressed down. The lid held for a moment, and Mark threw his weight to the bar. There was a squeal of protesting nails and the lid lifted back. Dusty reached forward to pull aside the oiled cloth covering and looked down at what the box held. Two faces looked up, eyes gleaming. They'd not expected the thing which lay exposed to their gaze.

Mark licked his lips. "It's a Gatling gun."

"Sure. About the smallest I ever saw," agreed Dusty.

The round, fat, gleaming body of the gun looked up at them, far smaller than the Gatling guns they'd become used to seeing. The models they knew were heavier pieces, mounted on artillery carriages. This was smaller and wouldn't weigh more than ninety or a hundred pounds. Reaching forward, Mark lifted the gun out of the box and Dusty saw the five-barrel muzzle staring at him. Then he dipped his hand into the box and took out a small, oilskin package. This contained a booklet giving instructions for the cleaning, maintenance, loading and firing of the new version gun. The first thing he saw, from the illustrations, was that the gun was mounted on a light tripod instead of the cumbersome carriage. Mark looked over Dusty's shoulder, then lowered the barrel and opened the second long box. The tripod was inside and Mark set it on to its leg, then mounted the gun barrel.

"Bust open the other boxes, Mark!" Dusty said, and he was not hiding his excitement now. Here was the means, much as he hated the thought of it, to break the Apache uprising.

Mark opened one of the larger, square boxes and looked at the round, drum-shaped thing inside. He lifted the metal drum out and saw a second underneath. It took him a moment to realize what they were. The old model Gatling used a straight magazine, but later types were fitted with the round drum, Accles Positive Feed magazine. Mark recalled having read something about this new magazine in a book. He lay the magazine back and opened another box to find, as he expected, bullets for the gun, long 45.70 cartridges of the Army pattern.

"We've got all we need," said Mark grimly. "If I can get it going in time."

"I reckon you'll have to," Dusty answered. "There's a book here that should tell you how to do it and you handled the Gatlings for the French at Saltillo. This one shouldn't be much different."

"Dusty!" Bronson's voice sounded faintly to them. "You'd best come up here and take a look, there's something happening."

Dusty paused. He wanted to help Mark, but his duty as leader in the fight came first. "I'll send Waco to help you, Mark. Pull the sheet back this side a mite but don't let the folks see what's inside."

Dusty left the wagon and called Waco over. The youngster did not know what to expect when he climbed into the wagon. What he saw made him whistle but he got no chance to ask questions. Mark pointed to the box which had held the tripod. "There's a cleaning rod inside the box of tools, boy. Get them out and let's make with the work."

Mark stripped off his shirt, for the wagon was hot with the canopy over it. He started to work on the gun. Mark knew something of Gatling guns for the French had two in Saltillo while Mark was serving General Sheldon, helping the Maximillian regime in their fight against Mexico. Mark was the officer who took care and maintained the guns, for the French did not. This new model was not different mechanically, the chief differences being the magazines and the firing handles. On the old model this was at the side while it was on the rear of the lighter type.

Dusty left Mark and Waco working to strip down, clean and prepare the gun for firing, working desperately against time and trying to get it ready for when the Apache attack began.

With the Ysabel Kid at his side Dusty hurried to the church and went through. He found Thornett keeping the women and children entertained with a display of card and sleight-of-hand tricks. The good doctor appeared to have been making the most of his time for several of the women, including Mrs. Millet, were holding bottles of the Superior Elixir.

There was no time to stop and see how Thornett was going on, and Dusty went up the stairs fast. They came through the trapdoor and on to the platform of the bell tower. Bronson's squad of sharpshooters were at their places, and the young soldier came to Dusty.

"Lobo Colorado's brought all his men in, from the slopes and the town. They're burning the houses at the back of town, working forward," he said.

"He's got them bringing blankets and things like that into the houses along the edge of the square," Molly went on.

The Kid and Dusty joined the girl, looking down at the scene of activity on the other side of the square. That the Apaches were burning the town did not surprise them, they expected it. They could not understand why the Indians were bringing a lot of burnable gear into the houses edging the square. The houses would burn well enough without any added help.

Then Dusty got it.

"Let's get down to the grounds, Lon," he snapped. "There's going to be the big attack real soon. Watch things, Chet, and let me know if anything's happening."

Even as Dusty spoke there showed a flicker of flame from one of the houses, smoke began to roll up, and the wind carried it towards the church wall. The Kid was next to see what was happening and followed Dusty down the stairs to the church. They went to the rear and found Ellwood sitting up, looking refreshed from his short sleep.

Quickly Dusty explained what was happening and Ellwood listened without a word. At last he spoke, "It looks bad. What do you think's our best chance?"

"I want you and two men you can trust in Big Em's wagon. Get it ready to shed that tarp faster'n I just said it."

"Have you something in mind, Captain?"

"Sure, Major. The lousiest, dirtiest trick I ever played in my life," said Dusty, and he was very sincere.

Dusty hated the thought of using that Gatling gun against the Apaches, even if it would save their own lives. The Gatling gun was bringing a new and deadly touch to war, wholesale slaughter. No longer could war be regarded as a chivalrous and gentlemanly business. Not when using mechanized weapons which could hurl out death as fast as a man could crank a handle.

Across the plaza house after house began to burn, the smoke rolling on the breeze, towards the walls of the church. This was Lobo Colorado's big medicine for defeating his white-eye enemies. His men would attack through the smoke which would blind the white men to them. They could take the church and kill the hated white-eye defenders with small loss to themselves. Loud would be the singing around the fires that night. Men lifting their voices and telling how the great war-chief Lobo Colorado brought victory to his people.

Dusty watched the smoke thickening and tried to

guess how long he had before the attack came. He went to the wagon and found Ellwood standing with four men at the end, ropes ran up, over the top and were fastened to the tarp, ready to drag it from the supports of the wagon.

"All set, Major?" asked Dusty.

"Ready, willing and able," Ellwood replied and smiled, it was strange to hear the words coming from his lips. "That youngster of yours has cut the ropes on the other side. It was safer that way."

Dusty nodded soberly. It was safer for Waco to slit the ropes from the inside than for a man to try and go around to the exposed plaza side and do it. Looking under the tarp Dusty asked. "How's it going, Mark?"

Mark turned, his magnificent torso bared, giant muscles writhing under the sweat-soaked skin. "We're not ready yet. Ask him to hold off for a spell."

"I'll do just that," Dusty promised and pulled out again.

The plaza was thickly covered in whirling clouds of smoke now, hiding the houses from Dusty's view. However Bronson's party could see over the smoke, and they gave a grim warning. Lobo Colorado's medicine was made. Even now the war-chief was going to the horse he used since the Kid shot down his first mount. Vaulting on to the horse Lobo Colorado waved his rifle and let out a wild scalp yell. Every other brave took up the cry.

"They'll be coming soon, Dusty!" Bronson yelled down.

"Tell all your bunch to try and get Lobo Colorado!" shouted the Kid. "Get him and the rest'll stop."

Mark and Waco worked fast but without flurry or fluster. They'd cleaned the gun and mounted it on the tripod and now were loading the magazines. Dusty entered the wagon to lend a hand, leaving the defense of the walls to the Kid. By now the defenders were beginning to realize what the smoke meant but there was no panic as yet. Every man held his weapon fully loaded and ready for use, the pitifully small supply of ammunition to hand for easy reloading.

Mark swung the first loaded magazine in to place on the gun and worked the cocking piece. It was not a moment too soon. From behind the smoke sounded a louder cry, then the thunder of hooves as the Apaches poured forward to the attack.

"The cover, Major. The cover!" Dusty roared.

Ellwood and his men threw themselves on the ropes, heaving with all their strength, coughing as the smoke filled their lungs. For a moment the tarp stuck, then it slid backwards off the supports and fell to the ground, revealing for the first time Big Em's load.

Lobo Colorado's attack was well planned, the mass of braves pouring forward, each man eager to get at the white-eyes in the church. They rode in a bunch, the cream of the bad-hat Apaches and they rode to their deaths.

Behind the squat, shining, yet somehow evil-looking gun Mark Counter waited. He ignored the spirit level and the elevating sights. They would be of no use to him at such close range. He glanced at Dusty and Waco, seeing they held spare magazines, then he roughly aligned the gun on the whirling smoke cloud and the vague shapes which were forming in it. Mark's face was grim as he began to whirl the handle, rotating the barrels and firing the Gatling gun.

The hideous chatter of the Gatling gun sounded loud, a harsh chattering rattle which wrote the finish to Lobo Colorado's dreams. Mark Counter whirled the handle and sent the lead pouring out, ripping into the oncoming Apaches. He used what was known as the swinging traverse, turning the gun on the pivot mounting instead of using the adjusting screws, pouring the 45.70 bullets in an arc of destruction. The charging Apaches never knew what hit them. The Gatling gun showed no discrimination as it cut down men and horses in its bloody swath.

The attack broke, no living man could stand up to that stream of never ending death which poured from the evil device on the wagon. The screams of the wounded and dying sounded loud, even louder than the yells and cheers of the white defenders as they brought their fire down into the smoke.

Then it was over and done with. The remaining Apaches shredding back into the smoke, through it and out of the town of Baptist's Hollow. The wind dropped as if knowing there was no further need for it to whirl the smoke across the plaza. The excited cheers of the defenders died away at the bloody horror which met their eyes. Never could any one of them have conceived what a single weapon could do. The Apache dead were strewn the width of the plaza, horses and men, with here and there a badly wounded brave feebly struggling.

A solitary shape came boiling through the fading smoke. A man with the headband of a chief and a bullet hole in his body. Straight for the wall he rode, his rifle crashing as he came. It was Lobo Colorado, his medicine shattered and spoiled, his dream of regaining the Apache lands broken.

Dusty's hands crossed, bringing out the matched Colts while Mark held his fire with the Gatling gun. Lobo Colorado threw three fast shots. One of the men with Ellwood went down. Then Dusty started to shoot.

He shot to kill and knew why Mark did not offer to use the Gatling gun.

Give Lobo Colorado his due. He'd fought his men like a warrior and a brave leader. He'd led them and taken his share of the risks and now he was beaten. Give him a warrior's death, not have him murdered by that foul machine which cut down all in its path.

Three times Dusty shot, the bullets struck home, rocking the Apache chief from his racing horse. Down to the bloody dirt of the plaza fell Lobo Colorado, rolled over once and lay still.

Cheers were ringing out from the walls. Women came running from the church, and every voice lifted in the praise of the man who saved them, who led them and who came out victorious in the end.

Suddenly, Dusty felt sickened by the whole business. His face was hard as he turned to the Kid and said, "Go put Lobo Colorado on a horse. Take him out into the hills and give him his warrior's due."

The Kid nodded, letting out his breath in a long sigh. This was the end of the Indian's way of life. His way of fighting could not stand up to a weapon such as the Gatling gun. Without a word he turned and went to where his white stallion stood, vaulted afork it and rode from the church grounds as eager hands dragged the wagon to one side.

Mark Counter and Dusty Fog looked at each other. The big Texan was soaked with sweat, and it was not all caused by the exertion of working the gun. Mark's face was pale and haggard under the dirt and two-day growth of whiskers. He looked at the Gatling gun in disgust.

"Damn it to hell, Dusty," he said. "I'll never feel clean again."

"I know how you feel," replied Dusty. "Throw a tarp over that damned gun. I never want to see one again."

Dusty swung down from the wagon and gripped Ellwood's hand. The big major watched the small Texan's face and knew something. No matter how a man looked at it. No matter that he probably never went into a church or offered a formal prayer, one thing was for sure. Captain Fog was a deeply religious man, and he hated what he'd just been forced to do.

Dusty watched the eager crowd swarming forward to congratulate him. Then he turned and looked at the burning town. The battle was over. The work of rebuilding would have to begin.

CHAPTER THIRTEEN

Madam Fiona Retires

"You did a fine piece of work, Captain Fog," the colonel commanding Fort Owen said, looking at the small Texan who sat facing him across the desk. "I wish there was some way the country could regard you. I'm promoting Bronson to sergeant-major and hope to promote Magoon as soon as possible. But it was you who made the defense possible and it is you who deserves——"

"I don't know how you get that idea, Colonel," Dusty replied. "Magoon and Chet Bronson were responsible for the defense. "I'm only a civilian, Colonel. I can't give orders to soldiers."

The colonel smiled. He knew this small Texan could walk out of the office and take command of nearly the whole of the 8th Cavalry if he felt like it. The men were talking of nothing other than Captain Dusty Fog, unless it was the fist-fight which was arranged to take place at the sutler's store that night.

"I'll pass that over. I know Magoon, he's braver than any lion but he hasn't the sense of leadership which made what you did possible."

Dusty moved uncomfortably in his chair. "You

said something about promoting Chet Bronson? I thought——"

"Lieutenant Torrance thought he was going to die of the fever and decided to clear his conscience. He talked to the surgeon-major who saw that General Crook got to know. Crook sent a rider with the order for Bronson's release and reinstatement with rank, the court-martial to be struck from his record. I thought all along there was more than met the eye to that business at Ramon's village, but the way the evidence was I couldn't do a thing."

"I'm pleased for Chet's sake," drawled Dusty. "Wondered why he wasn't taken to the Stockade."

"I'm also trying to get Harris's court-martial struck from his record and an award for his bravery," the colonel went on. "It's you I feel sorry for. There's nothing to show for what you did. Major Ellwood wrote a letter telling me everything but there's nothing I can do for you. President Grant has telegraphed and told me that the offer he made you at Moshogen still holds good."

"Thanks, but I'm a cowhand. And if I don't get on with what brought me out here I'm going to be an out-of-work cowhand. I'll be riding romorrow."

It was nearly three weeks since the fight at Baptist's Hollow. They'd been three hard-working weeks for Dusty. He stayed on in the town, organizing the burial parties, cleaning up details and rationing the food out until the Army arrived with supplies. His work was showing results, the town showing signs of being rebuilt, but it would be a cleaner, happy place. The ring-leaders of the old Baptist's Hollow were no longer there. Haslett, Millet and the good Deacon Routh were not of the kind to rebuild a shattered life and start again.

They'd left the town and headed east. Major Ellwood was still there, still town marshal, still mayor, but a wiser, happier and more tolerant man. Doc Thornett's show was given and proved a roaring success, not the least of which was Elwin, the Wonder Juggler.

Now at last it was over. The Gatling gun, brought out to Fort Owen in secret, to show the Apaches at a meeting, proved its worth in a savage and murderous manner. It proved to the Apaches once and for all time the futility of fighting the white man. It was now attached to the 8th Cavalry for use, and stood on its tripod mount by the gate of the fort, a bitter reminder to the beaten Apaches that their dream was over and done.

"I'm holding a ball for all officers and their wives tonight, Captain," the colonel remarked. "I'd like you and your three friends to be my guests."

"We'd like that, Colonel," answered Dusty. "If we can come in later. We've a previous engagement that might take some time."

"It wouldn't be to do with that fist fight Magoon and Tolitski arranged?"

"Hear tell that some of the officers' ladies don't cotton any to the idea of the fight," Dusty replied. "Fact being, there was some talk of their trying to make you stop it. So I'm not answering that." He paused and smiled, "It looks like that ball was arranged a mite sudden."

The smile was answered by a brief flicker across the colonel's grim face. "It was arranged as soon as I heard the date of the fight. And it was my wife's idea, not mine. Do you think Madam Fiona will win?"

"Why sure," replied Dusty, thinking of the secret training sessions Mark Counter had been giving Phyllis ever since the fighting at Baptist's Hollow ended.

"I've got ten dollars right here that says she doesn't."

"I'll cover it, Colonel."

The post sutler's store was crowded out, the troopers who could not get admission crowding outside and being given profane but exacting descriptions of what was going on within.

In the ring erected at the center of the room was being fought as hard and rough a fight as any of them were ever likely to see. For twenty-eight gruelling and hard fought rounds Phyllis and Big Em battled for the title of Female Pugilistic Champion of the World. The watching crowd were almost hoarse with their cheering, and all knew it would not be long before the fight was over, although the result was still far from certain.

One thing Phyllis knew, as she fought the long, hard rounds. She was getting too old for this kind of thing. Big Em was not a good fighter, just a wild swinger with the power of a mule-kick when she landed. A few years back Phyllis would have made mincemeat of the big woman. Right now Phyllis could hardly stand. Those wild swung punches took a lot of handling. It was only the training Mark managed to give Phyllis that saved her. She'd learned just enough to be able to avoid or ride the worst of the other woman's blows in the early rounds.

Phyllis staggered forward and swung a punch at the tottering Big Em. They both sank to their knees, resting their hands on the floor of the ring and not able to even hold their heads up. It was only Mark's training and the more expert seconding of Doc and Molly which got Phyllis this far. Now it looked as if she was finished and would not be able to toe the line for the next round. Thornett had one consolation. Big Em didn't look in any better shape to come out when time was called.

Mark Counter stood in Phyllis's corner as Thornett and Molly helped her back and sat her on the small stool. He watched them working on her and was unable to offer any advice which might help.

"It's no good, Mark," Thornett said grimly as he wiped the blood from Phyllis's face. "I'm not going to let her take any more punishment. We'll concede defeat."

Phyllis's eyes fluttered open, and she stared at Thornett through the puffed, swollen lids. Her bruised lips tried to say something, but failed.

"You'll lose about everything you've got, Doc," Mark drawled, for he knew how much Thornett was wagering on the fight.

"Better that than have Phyllis hurt any more," Thornett replied. "We'll still have the wagon and the acts. Being broke is something we've faced before. I ought to have put my foot down earlier and would have if we'd been married. Then, she won't marry a worn out old fake like me."

"Don't you be on that, Doc. I talked with her some, while I was helping her train for the fight. She'd marry you any time you want, would have years back but she always thought she wasn't good enough for you."

Thornett stared at Mark. All these long years, the one thing Thornett had hoped for was that Phyllis might agree to marry him. Yet he'd never worked up the courage to ask. He saw Phyllis looking up at him and gulped, for once his glib tongue stilled. Then he made his decision and spoke like a man:

"Phyllis, my dove, I'll marry you as soon as can possibly be arranged. We've a lot of time to catch up on."

Time was called at that moment, and Thornett

opened his mouth to say that the champion would not make the line. Phyllis pushed herself to her feet and moved forward. Somehow she looked revived and her hands were held as Mark showed her when she went to the ring center to toe the line.

The pride of Fort Owen staggered out. Big Em could barely stand, she was a bloody, battered hulk now for she'd learned a bitter lesson that sheer muscle could not match skill. For all that she was game and swung a wild haymaker which would have knocked Phyllis over the ropes had it landed.

Phyllis blocked the swinging blow, her right arm deflecting it over her shoulder. Her left fist sank into Big Em's ample middle bringing a gasp of pain and folding her over neatly. The right fist came up, it was a beautiful blow, an uppercut straight out of the book. Big Em's jaw took the punch, her head snapped back and she was lifted up until she was erect, then went on over to hit the floor with a crash that jarred the walls of the room.

"And that's that, Paddy," said Dusty Fog from where he sat in a place of honor at the ring side.

Magoon, face flushed with excitement, looked at the three smiling Texans and shook his head:

"Divil a bit of it, Cap'n darlin'. Old Em'll come skipping out of there like a fairy when time's called." He watched Big Em's seconds dragging her back to her corner. Anything less likely or fairylike was hard to imagine, but he raised his bull-voice in a bellow which rang over every other sound. "Come on now, Em. They can't hurt us."

For once in his life Magoon was wrong. Big Em was no nearer coming out on her own feet at the end of the minute than she'd been when her seconds carried her back at the end of the previous round. Time was called and Phyllis managed to get to her feet, then staggered to the ring center. If Big Em came out, Phyllis knew the fight was over. She couldn't do another thing. From the way she swayed it even looked as if she might not be able to keep her feet long enough to know.

Big Em's seconds played for time, trying desperately to get the woman to even show some signs. Then as the referee of the bout waved them to bring their fighter forward they shrugged and acknowledged defeat. For a second the room was silent as the soldiers saw their pride and joy lying beaten. Then the cheers rolled up and Phyllis was announced the winner. She did not hear the cheers, or Magoon's delighted yells for her legs gave way and she piled up on the floor.

It was the following morning, and there was a large group around the Thornett wagon. Janice and Elwin stood discussing plans for improving his act. Molly and Bronson, resplendent with the three bars and arc of silk of his new rank on his sleeve, were arranging to meet when his furlough came due in a month. Big Em and Magoon looked at Phyllis now Mrs. Erazmus K. Thornett. The wedding was over, and Dusty Fog found he'd added being best man to his numerous other achievements.

"When do I get another crack at the title, Madam?" asked Big Em.

"I'm afraid you do not, me dear," Thornett replied for his wife. "I cannot countenance my wife fist fighting. Therefore, as of now, Madam Fiona retired undefeated."

"Except the one time, way I recollect it," Dusty remarked. "Where're you going for the honeymoon, Phyllis?"

Phyllis leaned back against the wagon and threw back her head, easing her aching body. She looked at Thornett for guidance, but for once he did not appear to be able to decide.

"Any place the wagon can take us," Phyllis finally replied. "Except for Baptist's Hollow."

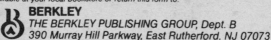